Lost and Found
In East Jesus

by David E. Peeler

CHIRON PUBLICATIONS • ASHEVILLE, NORTH CAROLINA

www.ChironPublications.com

Cover design by Matthew Norton
Interior design by Danijela Mijailovic
Printed primarily in the United States of America.

ISBN 978-1-63051-908-7 paperback
ISBN 978-1-63051-909-4 hardcover
ISBN 978-1-63051-910-0 electronic
ISBN 978-1-63051-911-7 limited edition paperback

Library of Congress Cataloging-in-Publication Data

Names: Peeler, David E, author.
Title: Lost and found in East Jesus / by David E Peeler.
Description: Asheville, North Carolina : Chiron Publications, [2020]
Identifiers: LCCN 2020049359 (print) | LCCN 2020049360 (ebook) | ISBN 9781630519087 (paperback) | ISBN 9781630519094 (hardcover) | ISBN 9781630519100 (ebook)
Subjects: LCGFT: Short stories.
Classification: LCC PS3616.E3259 L67 2020 (print) | LCC PS3616.E3259 (ebook) | DDC 813/.6—dc23
LC record available at https://lccn.loc.gov/2020049359
LC ebook record available at https://lccn.loc.gov/2020049360

Table of Contents

Dedication

For my wife Julie, whose faith in the unseen
gave me hope and opened my eyes to mystery.

A Cold Spring

Dell bent down as far as the pain in his back would allow and pressed the old towel against the base of the door. Rain that would have been snow the week before rolled down the mountain and turned frozen purity into pools of fertile brown. Other than a brief stint in the navy, he had spent his entire life on Taylor Mountain. After sixty-three years, this was the sort of spring he had come to expect: sudden and mud slick everywhere he turned. Before bright sprays of delicate mountain flowers colored the forest floor, an endless tide of water was required to thaw the earth and wake up the frozen ground. Making life was a wet, messy business, best overlooked until it was done.

Dell pressed one hand against his lower back for support and the other against the cabin door. He groaned as he levered himself upright. Once proud of his large frame, his heavy body had become a burden on joints that grew stiffer as the seasons passed. Like

"

the old tractor parked in the barn, he knew a life of hard work and the relentless flow of nature would claim him one day. Dell hoped that day would come with the suddenness of spring on the mountain and end as quickly as it began. The towel was already dark with water. He would have been willing to give the season its privacy had it not insisted on seeping under his front door to stain the carpet.

This was the first spring in years that Dell wasn't glad to see. Winters on the mountain were hard and lonely, even for a man who enjoyed his solitude. Warm weather meant that the summer folks from Florida would be back. The calls would start, slow at first, then two or three a day. They were more or less the same. The caller would ask how he was and if the winter had been a cold one, then the real reason for the call.

"Dell, we are planning on coming up this weekend. Can you get the house ready?"

His answer was always yes. The summer people paid him to say yes and Dell knew it. In winter, he made rounds in his pickup truck, checked that the houses were secure and undamaged. When the calls began to come in the spring, he would go to each house in turn to make it ready for its owner. It was light work to open windows, loosen closed water valves and see to it that gas still flowed to appliances and artificial logs. Dell also checked under porches and corners where he carefully laid traps. It wouldn't do for the Floridians or Texans to be greeted by the smell of a rotten mouse or a dead possum. If he did his work well, the homeowners would arrive to the illusion that winter did not exist. Other than a slight layer of dust, their retreat cabins were unchanged, waiting for their return.

The rhythm of the mountain had been the same since long before Dell was born. The highest spot on the rail line this side of Tennessee, the mountain had become an oasis in the midst of Appalachian poverty. A local architect made wealthy by the Vanderbilts constructed the Taylor Inn. After the massive Victorian structure with its rambling porches was completed, the cabins followed. His was one of the few families that had lived on the mountain before it became a resort. Generation after generation had broken themselves against the rocky soil to grow what amounted to survival rations. Dell was the last of those, an echo fading year by year into silence.

The train still came to the mountain, but it no longer stopped to disgorge linen-clad passengers. The old depot was a heap of falling-down bricks and rotten beams. Most of the cabins were gone, replaced by homes made from factory-cut logs and vista-facing panes of floor-to-ceiling glass. The mountain stood apart from the real world and the summer people liked it that way. It was Dell's job to make sure nothing disturbed their view.

He walked the few steps required to carry him from the front door to what passed for a kitchen, careful to keep his left leg as straight as the motion would allow. He wrapped both hands around the coffee mug that waited on the table and took one slow sip. Dell knew he would have to do something about Caleb and Charlotte before then.

Late Fall

The night they arrived Dell had finished locking up the last of the summer houses. The first snow was still weeks away, but already the days were growing short with the promise of long, cold nights to come. He stood on the front porch that was bigger than his home and looked down the mountain. Beyond the creek that was invisible in the darkness he saw light where there should not have been. The blue-white glow dipped and trembled, disappeared like a foxfire in the stories Dell's grandfather used to tell. The sound of voices and laughter drifted light, pressed thin on chilled air past leafless trees. Granddaddy said hill spirits could take the form of a young woman in a dress so white a blind man could see through it. Any man who followed one of those apparitions was led to the edge of a cliff or gully. When he finally reached out to take the vision in his arms, she disappeared, and the man fell to his death, done in by his own lust-filled loneliness. Beauty could kill, but only if you were fool enough to think you could make it your own.

The next morning Dell took the ax handle, wrapped at one end with camouflage duct tape, out of the truck's toolbox and placed it on the seat next to him. He flipped the switch on the flashing red light held by a magnet to the roof of the truck. The light was purchased at Home Depot and carried no authority, but Dell used it anyway. More than once the pulsing signal had been enough to frighten off wayward teenagers or wild ginseng poachers. He realized a long time ago his bark exceeded his bite. The ax handle was all but useless.

He drove slowly down the road from his cabin. The house nearest the spot where he had seen light gave him cause for concern. Most were well-maintained retreats, but not all. Occasionally an elderly retiree died in a faraway state and left property to a relative even farther away. Winters were harsh, but summer could be even harder on an empty house. Left barren, a place rotted quickly in the perpetual damp. Roofs covered by fallen leaves and moss sagged and eventually caved in.

The cabin where Dell stopped his truck was one of those forgotten places. Paint peeled away in red flakes from decayed boards, and the deck had long since collapsed, leaving only a skeletal frame. Metal lawn furniture, rusted and partially sunken into the earth, gave the place the appearance of forgotten battlefield. A family had once laughed and played on this ground, escaped from whatever burdens waited for them below the mountain. Now the house was nothing more than an unintended headstone that marked the grave of abandoned memories.

"Shit."

The pickup truck parked in front of the shack looked as if it had been cobbled together from the same decayed scrap metal that punctuated the yard. Smoke curled from the stone chimney at corner of the house. Dell could tell from the color and thickness of the plume that whoever was inside was burning gathered branches instead of seasoned firewood. No one came to Taylor Mountain by accident. The exit that led to the labyrinth of gravel roads was virtually invisible from the highway, barely a wide spot in the trees along a corridor of pitiless stone. Dell had never encountered a wandering squatter who happened upon an abandoned house and decided to take up residence. Until now he would not have believed such a circumstance was possible, but what else could this be?

The old shack was long past the point that it could serve as a decent home. Nothing but desperation remained in those walls.

Dell hesitated for a moment then blew three short blasts with horn of his truck. There were more social ways to greet whoever was inside but none that would allow him an easy escape. He was about to signal a second time when movement from behind the house stopped his hand. The boy who appeared from the rear of the cabin wore a faded black T-shirt with a Jack Daniel's label and work pants that were torn and frayed. Dell watched him stiffen at the site of the flashing light as he walked closer to the truck. He stopped a few feet away and inspected the rotating signal then looked at Dell. Put at ease by what he saw, the young man continued his approach. Before Dell could speak, an open hand pushed through the truck window. Between each knuckle of the offered hand were tattooed letters so blurred that Dell could not make out their message.

"I'm Caleb. Do you live around here?"

Dell could not refuse a handshake and was forced to meet the stranger on equal terms.

"I'm Dell. I live up the mountain, just after the first big curve." Dell tried to form a question of his own, but Caleb beat him to it with the ease of a used car salesman accustomed to controlling the flow of a conversation.

"You must live here year-round. Most of these places are empty by now. How do you keep your place warm?"

Dell heard himself answer, as if the words were spoken by someone else, a voice on the radio. "Woodstove mostly, but I have one of those new ceramic heaters, too, for when it gets really cold."

"That's smart. We might have to get one of those. I got a fire going last night but I haven't had a chance to pile up much wood. Might not before it gets real cold."

Dell was about to ask questions of his own when the front door of the cabin groaned open on long-unused hinges. Caleb, one arm inside the truck past his elbow, waved with the other toward the house. "Charlotte come here and meet our new neighbor."

Charlotte was beautiful in a way Dell felt more than understood. Tall and slender with straight black hair, she reminded him of a princess he had seen once in a play. He couldn't remember the story, just the end when the theatre went black as the girl died. Caleb stepped back from the truck and wrapped his arm around the girl's waist. "Charlotte, this is Dell."

Charlotte smiled and extended a hand through the window of the truck. "Nice to meet you."

Dell took the girl's hand and just as quickly released it. Freed from Caleb's control, Dell recovered himself. "Are you planning on staying up here? I take care of most of the houses on the mountain when the summer folks are away. This place is in pretty bad shape."

Caleb was about to answer when Charlotte leaned into the window blocking him from view. "It's my great-aunt's place. She's in a nursing home over in Asheville. She told us we could live here if we fixed it up for her."

Dell nodded and reached for the truck's ignition but didn't turn it. He wanted to ask the girl for her aunt's name, but an instinct close to pity stopped him. "Well, I'll be on my way. Good luck with that place. Not much there to work with."

Charlotte stepped back and pressed her hip against the boy's. "You would be surprised. Caleb will work miracles with what we have here."

Dell started the truck and pulled away. They stayed next to each other and waved until he thrust one arm out the window in return. Her story wasn't true. Dell knew there was no elderly aunt in a nursing home or at least he was fairly certain there wasn't. He was glad for the doubt and the freedom it gave him to do nothing. The boy seemed fragile, desperate; not in himself but in the way he clung to the girl. A lifetime spent on his own had given Dell the opportunity to understand the things he couldn't have and why he couldn't have them. Caleb would have to learn for himself.

Several days passed without Dell seeing either Caleb or Charlotte. He drove past the shack a few times on his rounds and each time the truck was absent, but there were signs that the house was still occupied. Faded bedsheets hung in the windows as makeshift curtains, and a blue tarp was stretched over the frame of the collapsed porch to cover a haphazard woodpile. Dell opened the front door of his house and stood outside. The air was wet and cold. It made his knee and back ache. There was no reason to be outside, but the presence of the young couple unsettled him like the broken barking of a distant dog on an otherwise quiet night. The only sound should have been the rattle of wind through bare tree branches, but Dell heard something else: string-picked cords accompanied by a human voice that faltered to laugh then resumed, glided over stone and cold earth up the mountain.

The drive to the cabin was short, too short for him to change his mind and turn back. Caleb and Charlotte sat on the edge of a fire pit constructed from piled stones. She was wrapped up to her neck in an old quilt, legs folded into a resurrected lawn chair. Caleb sat on a large stump, his body bent over a guitar, a case of beer by one leg. Dell slung his stiff knee out of the truck and broke the silence that followed his arrival.

"I heard you playing up at my place. Is it all right if I join you?"

Caleb spoke, "Take a seat anywhere you can find a dry spot. You want a beer?"

Dell accepted the beer with a nod and eased himself down on the stump on the opposite side of the fire from Caleb. "What were you playing?"

"I don't really play. I just like to pick this thing sometimes."

Charlotte pushed herself above the quilt, caused the decayed chair to rasp like metal under a file. "That's not true. Caleb can really play, and he sings too. One day we're going to Nashville."

The pitch of her voice was familiar, like a guitar string pulled too tight. Dell knew the sound of hope stretched over a lifetime of bad luck when he heard it. He'd been wrong. The boy wasn't clinging to something he knew he shouldn't have. There was nothing for both of them. It was an old story: scrape together two piles of misery and pray for a miracle. Dell knew better. A burden shared wasn't a burden halved; it was just more to be buried under.

"Don't be shy. Play something. Take my mind off what this stump is doing to my back."

Caleb looked at Charlotte and lowered his head and started to play. This time there were no fits and starts, no laughter. The song wasn't an old one, "Seven Bridges Road," though Dell realized it was probably a classic to both of them. The way Caleb sang it, high and clear, felt old like the ballads Dell's grandmother sang. Dell struggled to name the tightness in his chest that felt like he was pulled out of himself and a world of mourning pushed in at the same time. Something timeless and not of his own making whispered to him between the notes.

****

"Dell, you look terrible."

"At my age, terrible is the only way I look."

The old man looked up from the workbench where he sat, bent over the carburetor of his aging tractor. The machine had struggled to start and even stalled out a few times. Dell knew snow was on its way and he would need the machine to work reliably to clear the roads. Charlotte stood in the doorway of the barn he used as workshop. With the sun at her back, he could only see the shape of her, and it seemed as if a shadow spoke to him.

She walked over and swatted him on the shoulder, hand limp and laughing. "That's not what I meant. Your beard is over your neck, and I can't see your ears. When was the last time you had a haircut?"

"It's been a while, not that it matters. There's nobody up here to see me. I usually get it cut before the summer folks start coming back."

"I'm not nobody, and I see you every day. Why don't you let me cut it for you? I cut Caleb's hair for him."

Dell glanced up at her and then turned back to the oil-stained tractor parts on the bench. It was true. She did see him every day. After their first visit, Dell found himself stopping by the abandoned cabin more and more often until it became a nightly ritual. Most nights they gathered around the fire, and Caleb did most of the talking or forced Dell to do so with an endless string of questions. Charlotte hardly spoke, though she laughed often and called them both out on their more obvious lies. On nights when his back or knee hurt too much to make the trip down the hill they came to him and watched T.V. instead of listening to Caleb play. Dell had stopped caring if they had a right to be in the old shack or not.

"Do you know what you're doing?"

"Of course, I do. Besides, if it looks bad, there won't be anyone to see but me and Caleb, and I will make him promise not to laugh."

"All right then. Where do we do it?"

Charlotte grinned and extended both hands toward him if as trying to hold a disobedient dog in place. "Stay right there. I will get my scissors and be right back. Don't move."

She was back sooner than Dell would have thought possible with scissors, a ragged towel, and plastic pocket comb. Charlotte guided him to the center of the shop directly under a bare light bulb and wrapped the towel around his neck. She ran her fingers through his hair a few times then stepped back to study him, her head angled to one side. She started to cut slowly at first, then faster, more confident. Neither one of them spoke.

It had been a long time since Dell had been this close to a woman. Charlotte's touch, against his scalp and the back of his neck was a brush of memory, desire without urgency. The summer people sometimes asked if he ever got lonely on the mountain by himself. He always said no and meant it. When Charlotte began to cut the coarse hair of his beard, her hand rested against his face. Dell closed his eyes and let her work.

Mid-Winter

Dell pulled the handle on the faded recliner that after more than a decade of use retained an imprint of his body even when he wasn't in it. He closed his eyes, his head dropped back, and he folded his hands under the crease of his stomach. Outside the world as far as it'd ever mattered to him was buried in snow pushed by a warning wind. The sun was gone, elbowed back by low clouds as impenetrable as stone. Out there it was hard, but Dell didn't care.

"You're not supposed to look like that until after we eat."

Dell opened his eyes to look at Charlotte where she stood at the foot of his recliner. Her hair was pulled back in a long braid that uncovered the slender line of her neck. Over her clothes she wore his carpenter's smock in place of an apron, the pockets cleared of debris to make room for the few kitchen implements Dell owned. She had insisted on a Christmas meal a few days ago, then lapsed into an embarrassed silence. Dell visited Caleb and Charlotte often since that first night around the fire but never went inside their broken-down cabin. They had running water, he made certain of that. It was a simple matter of turning the valve that connected the shack to the community cistern. He was equally certain they had no electricity. When he suggested they cook the meal at his home, Charlotte wrapped her arms around him. Dell could not remember the last time another body had been this close to his.

"I'm just comfortable. There's nothing wrong with that. Besides, you told me to stay out of your way."

Charlotte waved the spoon she held in his direction. "I didn't tell you to stay out of the way. I said I wanted to do all of the cooking."

Dell watched her walk back to the kitchen before he closed his eyes again.

"Where's Caleb? I haven't seen him today."

Charlotte answered with her back to him, eyes on a pot that simmered on the stove. "He's working on something at the cabin. He'll be here in time for dinner." She had lied to him before, about her aunt. He knew that, but not because the lie was badly told. This time she wasn't trying, as if Charlotte wanted him to doubt her.

"Did you two have a fight?"

"No. He's just upset. He said he needed some time alone to think, but he'll be here for dinner." The way she repeated the phrase made it sound like a child's wish or a prayer.

"What's he upset about? Maybe I can help." Dell knew as soon as he said the words, they were empty. He could give them a place to have Christmas dinner but not much else. If they needed money or decent place to live, he didn't have it, not for both of them.

Charlotte turned away from the stove and faced him. The way she held herself pressed back against the oven door, feet and legs angled into the floor as if only her body held up the entire house, made him feel the need to sit upright and lean into what she was about to say. He fought the urge, kept his hands folded in front of him, feet in the air. If he sat up, whatever was wrong became his too. He wasn't sure he wanted that.

"If I tell you, you have to promise not to say anything to Caleb."

"All right. What happens between the two of you is none of my business anyway. There's no need for me to shoot off my mouth."

"I told Caleb this morning that we are going to have a baby. It hasn't been long, I don't think. I thought he would be happy, like it was a Christmas present. He was at first, then he got worried. I'm worried too and scared but I think everything will be all right. Don't you think everything will be all right? Everything happens for a reason, doesn't it?"

Charlotte was older than many of the girls Dell grew up with when they had their first baby. He guessed she was somewhere in her early twenties, Caleb too. Of course, those girls were married, and their husbands worked in factories or in a family business. That wasn't the only difference, though. Caleb and Charlotte seemed younger than they were and much younger than the people he'd known as a young man. By the time he was Caleb's age, Dell had finished a stint with the Navy and had come home to work his family's farm when there was still a farm to work. The world changed while Dell was alone on the mountain. People that he would have considered grown remained childlike in so many ways. Maybe everything did happen for a reason, but he'd given up trying to understand what those reasons were a long time ago.

"Sure honey, everything will be fine. Caleb will come around. Raising a baby is a big responsibility. That's why I never had any myself. He'll be here in time for Christmas dinner, and everything will be all right."

Late Winter

More than a week had passed since Dell had seen either Charlotte or Caleb. The snow had come late this winter, then slammed into the mountain like a fist. After decades of winters, his house was as secure against the cold as it could be. The heat from the wood stove and the stone fireplace kept him comfortable. The old shack was another story. More gaps than boards and no real insulation meant that Caleb and Charlotte were suffering even if they were surviving. Dell pulled on heavy rubber boots and settled the weight of his wool coat on his shoulders. They needed him.

The distance from his place to the cabin was less than a quarter of a mile, but the steep angle of the road and the calf-deep snow left Dell in agony. Under the layer of snow, the road was frozen solid. Even with four-wheel drive, his truck would have slipped until it came to rest in a ditch or slid off the mountain altogether. When Dell finally reached the shack, he was out of breath and his knee throbbed.

As he neared the front door, Dell heard a sound that caused him to stop and listen over the sound of his own labored breathing. The walls of the broken-down house were thin, and all but whispers could be heard through them. Inside someone sobbed in ragged gasps. Dell was certain it was Charlotte until he heard a raised voice that he knew was hers.

"For God's sake, how long are you going to do that. Shut the hell up. Caleb, how much longer do we have to keep this little bitch here? I can't take much more."

Dell listened, perfectly still except for the twisting sensation in his stomach, to Caleb's equally angry reply. "I don't know Charlotte. They were supposed to pick her up two days ago, but this damn snow is impossible. We have to keep her here until someone can come get her."

Dell knew he should do something, at least go to the door and try to see who they had inside. He started toward the cabin but stopped after a single step. What could he do? Whatever was happening in there, he was just an old man with a ruined leg and a flashing light on the back of his truck. If the girl they had inside was in trouble, there was nothing he could do to help her except get himself hurt in the process. Dell could still hear sobbing as he walked slowly back up the frozen road. He kept moving even when the pain in his leg pleaded for him to stop.

****

Dell pulled on his wool watch cap, a relic from his navy days, and stepped out of his front door. The trees rose, tall and sudden, and, even leafless, blocked out the horizon. Unlike the homes built by the summer people, the old farmhouse had not been built with a view in mind. His grandfather's concerns had been of a more practical nature, easy access to water and flat ground that harbored as few rocks as possible. It had been two days since his aborted attempt to check on Caleb and Charlotte. He tried to convince himself that there was nothing to worry about, that his imagination had simply gotten the better of him. Dell would have succeeded had it not been for one thing. Charlotte's voice still haunted him. He knew she could get angry. Every young couple fought, and Dell had witnessed her give Caleb a tongue lashing on more than one occasion. What happened at the cabin two days ago was different. More than the stranger's sob, the cruelty in her voice turned him away. That voice made him afraid.

His thoughts were interrupted by the distinct crunch of footsteps in the unpacked snow. Dell didn't have to wait long before the source of the footsteps became visible on the road. Caleb wore a black hooded jacket that was inadequate for the cold and his usual brown work pants. Dell considered retreating into the house but just as quickly realized it wouldn't do any good. Where else would he be in weather like this. Instead, he stood and waited for the boy to labor his way through the snow.

Caleb threw up one hand in greeting before he joined Dell on the porch. Dell had never seen the boy completely clean-shaven or wearing anything other than clothing that Goodwill would have refused, but today he looked even worse than usual. Caleb's eyes were sunken and dark, and a thin stream of mucus made its way toward his winter cracked lips. Most pitiful of all to Dell were the boy's boots. The seams were split in several places and the soles held on by duct tape. Dell's family had been poor when he was growing up, but it had been a point of pride with his father to ensure that all his children had decent shoes to wear. Anything else would have been an irretrievable loss of human dignity.

Under normal circumstances Dell would not have allowed a stranger, much less a friend, to stand outside in the cold, but today was different. Once a haunt crossed a doorsill it could be difficult to remove. Dell had enough ghosts of his own without borrowing any from the boy. He waited in silence for Caleb to speak.

"Listen Dell, I need your help. Well, really, Charlotte does, but I'm the one doing the asking."

Things must be bad at the cabin. Dell had never known Caleb to ask for anything directly. His usual approach was a steady stream of banter that wound itself around you until whatever he wanted seemed like your idea in the first place.

"What sort of help?"

Caleb looked Dell in the eyes when he spoke, another sure sign of desperation.

"It's the road. I know Charlotte's not very far along but if something happened with the baby, we couldn't get out for help. I tried to tell her everything would be all right but she's working herself to death. If you could take that old tractor and clear the road, it would put her mind at ease. You wouldn't have to go far. Just down to where the road is paved. I would do it for you but I don't know how to drive that thing."

Dell turned his head and looked at the line of tracks the boy had left in the snow. The road needs to be plowed, he knew that. In fact, the only thing that had kept him from it this long was the pain the old machine caused in his back. The old man knew there was more to Caleb's urgency than the boy was telling, but absent a clearer reason, he had no cause to refuse.

"All right, you head on back, and I'll be down in bit to plow the road. It might take me a while to get that old tractor warmed up and moving, but I'll be there."

Caleb nodded and slapped Dell on the shoulder before he started back the way he had come.

"Thanks, Dell. I knew you'd come through for us. Charlotte will be grateful, and so am I."

Dell was prepared for this moment. He carefully tended the old Ford tractor all year long to ensure that when called upon, the antique machine would respond. There were few places in his life where Dell allowed himself anything that approached senti-mentality, but the tractor was one of them. The machine had belonged to his father, the result of a lifetime of saving and doing without. The old man died less than a year after he bought it at an auction in Waynesville. When he cranked the engine, Dell thought he could feel the worn-out farmer smiling down on him from whatever heaven took men who never went to church but prayed every day with their hands in God's dirt.

The sound of the engine, metallic and guttural, struck the winter silence like a Bible slammed against a pulpit. Dell gritted his teeth as the vibrations from the engine traveled through the tractor's dented metal frame and up his spine. Newer models were built for the operator's comfort with padded seats, cup holders and shocks to smooth the ride. The only comfort his father's Ford offered was the comfort of not doing back-breaking work by hand. Dell realized a long time ago that the true measure of luxury is the amount of misery an object relieves.

With the engine warmed up, the tractor moved easily through the snow. Its weight and large tires kept it stable on the roadbed. Dell was relieved when he reached the shack and saw that no one was outside. He wanted to complete the task of scraping the road as quickly as possible and avoid a situation that might force him to ask questions that he didn't want answered. A sharp push against a lever as stiff as his own joints lowered the plow onto the snow encrusted road. Dell eased the throttle open and smiled with satisfaction as dry drifts parted in front of him and left exposed roadbed in his wake. His satisfaction was short-lived.

"Son of a bitch."

Dell slapped his hand against the steering wheel of the tractor. He immediately regretted the gesture that sent waves of pain up his cold, numbed fingers. From where he sat on the tractor he could see that the paved main road had been scraped clean and salted by the county snowplows. Less than a hundred yards from where from where gravel and blacktop met, a long dead oak, burdened by the weight of the snow, had fallen across his path. All his effort had been for nothing as long as the decayed carcass remained in place. He briefly considered ramming the tree with his plow but just as quickly dismissed the idea. If some part of the fallen skeleton remained solid, it would easily tear apart the front end of the ancient machine. There was only one option open to him. He would have to return with a chainsaw and cut the wooden corpse into manageable pieces that he could then drag off the road. There was a time when Dell could have accomplished the task on his own, but those days were long past. He would need Caleb's help to get the work done.

Dell stopped the tractor in front of the broken-down cabin and waited. He knew that anyone inside could hear the growl of the engine through the thin walls. He hoped that someone, preferably Caleb would emerge to greet him. When several minutes passed with no sign of movement inside the shack, Dell groaned and eased himself down from the tractor. Normally, he would have cut off the engine to conserve fuel, but the old Ford had a mind of its own and could prove difficult to restart. Some instinct told him that he might want to leave in a hurry, and Dell didn't want the cantankerous machine to slow his exit.

The swaybacked steps and decayed front porch of the cabin were piled high with snow. Dell was careful with his footing to avoid a fall. He could smell the oily scent of a kerosene heater burning inside. Even with the heater wide open and a fire in the wood stove, he knew the cabin must be unbearably cold. If for some reason

Caleb and Charlotte were forced to leave the mountain, it was difficult to imagine they would land somewhere more miserable than this. He knocked on the front door that rattled on its rusted hinges and listened for movement inside. At first there was nothing. Then the sound of muffled voices and footsteps creaked over the cabin floor.

Caleb opened the door and looked at Dell as if he didn't recognize him before he spoke.

"Oh, Dell. I wasn't expecting you. I heard the tractor go by earlier. Is the road clear?"

Caleb kept the door almost entirely closed, with only his head outside like a frightened prey animal inspecting the world for danger before leaving its warren. Dell was about to explain about the tree when something shoved Caleb from behind and pushed his face into the door frame. Caleb made an inarticulate sound of pain and grabbed his face. Free from his grip, the door opened wider. A young girl with blond hair and blue eyes that were too wide for her sunken face stood behind him. Her ragged dress was too thin for the winter cold, and Dell could see that on her feet she wore a pair of rubber garden clogs that left her ankles exposed. The moment the girl made eye contact with Dell she began to speak in a language he had never heard before, repeating the same phrase over and over again. Even though he couldn't understand the words, he knew a plea for help when he heard it.

The girl tried to push past Caleb and reach Dell, but something stopped her. Charlotte stood behind her, eyes wide with anger, her teeth bared. She grabbed the girl by the tattered dress and pulled her back into the darkness of the cabin.

"Caleb, you idiot, get her back to her room before she runs out into the snow and freezes to death."

Caleb turned without a word and walked back into the house. Charlotte stood alone in the doorway with her eyes locked on Dell. The tension in her arms and neck reminded him of a cornered animal in the seconds before it attacked to fight for its life. He stepped back and barely caught himself before falling down the snow slick stairs. When Charlotte spoke, her voice was a ragged threat.

"Go, Dell. Just go."

The old man turned and walked back to the tractor glad that the engine was still running.

Spring

Dell lifted his coffee cup to his lips and made a sour face. The cup had gone cold while he worried. Charlotte had told him to go, and he stayed gone. Leaving people alone and being left alone were familiar to him, a rhythm of emptiness he fell into with practiced ease. A few days of solitude, and it was if Caleb and Charlotte never existed, a pair of specters conjured by the mountain that faded in the light of day. Like all haunts, their passing left a mark, a whisper that dogged his steps and followed him to his bed at night.

Alone in his house with nothing to do but feed the wood stove and himself, he thought often about that day in the snow. He tried to convince himself that there was an explanation, something he didn't understand that could make sense of it. No matter how hard he tried, the sick feeling that settled low in his gut that day remained. Someone had been left to suffer because he was afraid.

Now spring was on the way. Alone, holed up from the cold, he could pretend there was nothing to worry about, nothing terrible happening in that broken-down place, but the summer people were coming. One of them was bound to notice people living in the old cabin, people who clearly did not belong. Dell pictured the phone call to the sheriff, Caleb arguing with a sheriff's deputy then thrown to the ground, faced pressed into the dirt by a uniformed knee. They would search the house. The girl was always the same, dirty and thin, found locked in a closet. After that, there would be questions: Had he seen anything, what did he know about Caleb and Charlotte? Sometimes the scene ended with him in handcuffs, guilty of collusion and clear cowardice. Dell knew he had to convince them to leave before someone else did.

It was Charlotte who saved him, appearing at the door in a dripping red poncho, head bent against the rain. He heard the wooden gate that led to his house groan open then crash shut on its spring. Charlotte didn't knock. Instead, she called out through the door. "Dell, it's me. Can I come in?" Dell didn't move. He considered saying nothing, waiting for her to leave, then realized this might be the best chance he would have.

"Come on in."

She opened the door, had to push with her shoulder when the wet towel jammed against the floor. Dell stayed at the table and watched her remove the dripping sheet of thin plastic. He tried to remember if he'd ever seen a prettier girl and couldn't remember that he had. Maybe if she didn't look like that, none of this would've happened. He would've thrown them out that first day. He decided that wasn't it. He liked the boy, too, enjoyed listening to him sing and play.

Charlotte smiled down at him, as she pushed a strand of wet hair away from her face. "We've been missing you. I thought I would stop by and see how you were doing."

The now familiar twisting in his stomach was back, made worse by how good it felt to be near Charlotte again. Underneath the red poncho she wore a white sweater that accentuated rather than hid the bump at her midsection and a pair of new blue jeans. It was the first time that Dell had seen her in clothing that was new. Part of him wanted to stand up and embrace her, welcome the smiling girl in white into his home. Instead, Dell tightened his grip on the coffee cup and forced himself to remember the other Charlotte, the one who stood in her doorway and told him to go.

"Charlotte, I'm too old for pretending. You and Caleb are doing something I want no part of. Things change on this mountain come springtime. The folks who own the big houses come back. Don't think they won't notice you, because they will. They'll notice and then they'll start asking me questions. I won't lie for you Charlotte. I like you and Caleb, but this is the only living I've got. The summer folks will blame me for not doing something about the two of you sooner, and I can't have that."

Charlotte continued to smile, but her entire body tensed, hands closed over the slight swell of her stomach. "I don't know what you're talking about. That girl you saw was a friend of ours. She was just freaked out by being trapped in the snow. Her family came for her the same day. Caleb and I aren't up to anything."

It was there again. The same satin tone from the first time she lied to him and meant it to stick. If she had broken down, cried, told him the truth and blamed Caleb, he would have believed her and tried to help. Now there was nothing he could do.

"Charlotte, I don't want to hear any more. You and Caleb need to go and soon. If you leave now, there won't be any fuss, and I won't say a word about y'all being in that old shack all winter. You can disappear like you've never seen this mountain. If you wait, it won't be that easy."

Charlotte smiled at Dell, but her eyes were the same as that day in the snow, hard and dangerous. "OK, Dell. Have it your way. Caleb and I were planning on leaving soon anyway. We saved up enough money over the winter to get a new start in Nashville. I guess I was just hoping we could part as friends."

Dell looked down at the brown liquid in his cup, not all that different from the color of the mud running down the sides of his mountain home. It was safer to look there than at Charlotte. If he looked at her, he knew his eyes would betray him.

"If you and Caleb leave soon, today or tomorrow, we will part as friends. After that I can't make any promises."

Charlotte didn't say another word. She pulled on the red poncho, opened the door and stepped outside into the rain. Dell started to watch her go but he couldn't. Instead, he rose slowly from the chair, careful as always with his knee and back. Spring would come, wet and insistent, sowing life and all its complications. He couldn't stop what happened in the world outside, but he didn't have to let it in either. Dell pushed the sodden towel back against the crack in the door, ready to wait out another season.

The Fall of the Archangel

The contortionist on top of the coffin was well past her prime. An outsider would never have noticed the slight tremors in her shoulders or the pain-deepened creases at the corners of her eyes. All a townie would have seen was the graceful motion of her sequin-covered body as she bent and twisted on top of the box that was carried on the shoulders of four large men. The residents of Gibbtown, the freaks, the fire eaters, lion tamers and clowns, noticed. They saw the effort it took for the retired center ringer to balance on hands bent by arthritis and they loved her for it. The man in the tapered wooden box, cut in the style of a Wild West coffin and painted with a pair of angel wings would have loved it, too. Ellis Teller, the Archangel of the High Wire, had devoted himself to the circus. To have his coffin serve as stage would have suited him just fine. Even in death the show must go on.

Reverend Talbot Jones stood at the head of the open hole that would soon receive the body of the Archangel. Ellis had been a friend, and the pastor fought back tears as the procession wound closer. The Gibbtown cemetery, like everything else in this corner of West Florida, resisted what the rest of the world would call normal. There were no orderly straight rows of virtually identical headstones here. The circus folk buried their fallen in an ever-increasing series of concentric circles, meant to resemble the rings where they lived their lives. It had occurred to Talbot on more than one occasion that the Gibbtown cemetery was likely to be one of the liveliest places on earth when the day of resurrection finally arrived. Newly risen acrobats, animal trainers, and knife throwers could perform their routines without fear of injury to their eternal bodies.

The unusual placement of the headstones did make for an easy route of ingress for the Archangel's pallbearers. Talbot averted his eyes as the four men carrying the coffin sidestepped the granite foreleg of a life-sized circus pony. He was certain the sudden movement would topple the contortionist from her perch. After six years as the only clergy person in Gibbtown, Talbot should have known better. The performer moved in a gravity-defying slow motion with no more apparent effort than if she were standing on solid ground. The rocking coffin was no more likely to dislodge her than a gentle breeze could move a mountain.

Talbot made an unnecessary adjustment to his clergy stole, handmade by a prisoner, and straightened his cassock. There was a time when his attire, unusual for a United Methodist minister, would have made him uncomfortable, but those days were long past. The cassock had once been ordinary enough, though more Catholic in appearance than most Protestant ministers would have allowed. Talbot preferred its slim lines over the billowed folds of a preaching robe as a matter of vanity. His stick-thin frame looked absurd wrapped in all that cloth, like a Halloween ghost come to life, all neck and with an overly large head. The other features of his clergy attire were far from ordinary.

Shortly after his arrival in Gibbtown, one of the beloved circus elephants, a matron named Bess, had died of extreme old age. The entire community mourned as if one of their own grandmothers had been taken from them. Talbot always chose to err on the side of compassion rather than rigid theological correctness in his pastoral duties. In the hope of providing an outlet for the town's grief, he approached the elephant's trainer and offered to hold a memorial service for the fallen animal. Nearly the entire town attended the service, which required the use of a large crane for the interment, and in one heartfelt gesture of compassion, the new pastor won over his new community. The vestments he now wore were a gift presented several weeks after Bess's funeral. The elephant trainer's wife sewed ruby red sequins onto the cuffs, collar, and hem of his cassock. She also made the stole, white robed angels that wept on a field of black. Each angel had the face of a clown, with no two faces alike. The additions to his vestments gave Talbot the appearance of a religious ringmaster, a role that in this place was held in absolute reverence.

In spite of their difficult burden, the pallbearers finally arrived at the foot of the grave. The Florida heat hung in the air like the breath of an unconscious drunk, damp and thick, and the four men who carried the coffin blinked as sweat rolled into their eyes. Their destination reached, the men made no move to put the casket down. The contortionist continued to bend and twist, her body coiling around itself as if she were made of living water rather than flesh and bone. With a performer's instinct for the emotions of a crowd honed to perfection by decades on the road, the woman in red sequins intensified her movements until the last of the mourners gathered at the graveside. In one flawless motion, she moved into a perfect handstand in spite of the pain the position must have caused her and somersaulted off the coffin. There was no applause this time, but the absolute silence of the graveside spectators was charged with the energy of restrained alleluias.

Talbot waited until the contortionist took her place among the other funeral-goers, and the coffin was placed on its cradle over the open grave before he spoke. "Friends, we are gathered here in our shared grief. We are also gathered here in our shared and certain hope. Our hope rests in the grace of God and the promise of the resurrection of the body. Just as Ellis Teller, the Archangel, soared in life, he now takes flight in the eternal presence of his creator."

The graveside service concluded with words as familiar as they are misunderstood. "Earth to earth, ashes to ashes, dust unto dust." Talbot knew that most people took that ancient proclamation as one more sign of the nature of the Christian faith, a proclamation of the frailty and futility of human life. Nothing could be farther from the truth. Dust in the hands of God was the stuff of life, pure potential awaiting the breath of the creator to live again. To consign the remains of the dead to ash and dust was the proclamation of a new beginning, not the pronouncement of a final and therefore pointless end. Talbot always attempted to infuse his voice with hope as he said those words and to allow that hope to linger in his eyes as he greeted each of the family members in turn at the conclusion of the service. Normally he moved to the person most closely related to the deceased first, but the odd formation of the cemetery this time forced him to move in the reverse order. He shook hands with a man he had only just met that day, a distant cousin of the deceased and his wife before he came to those dearest to the fallen angel. The performer's twin children, Jackson and Zelda Teller, sat so close together that their bodies touched at their shoulders, hips, and knees. Blond and muscular, they both mirrored their father and had become exceptional athletes in their own right. Though both had performed with the Archangel, he had insisted that they attend college before joining the family business on a permanent basis. In just a few months they would leave Gibbtown and their widowed mother. Talbot clasped the hand of both twins and moved on.

Martha Teller, the Archangel's wife was the picture of understatement in town that thrived on the extravagant. Her dark hair was pulled back in an elegant but simple bun that suited the plain black dress she wore. The only jewelry she displayed was her gold wedding band that was scuffed with decades of wear. Petite to the point of fragility, either one of her children could have lifted her as a prop for one of their routines. Like many people in Gibbtown, Martha Teller was more than what she seemed. She eloped with the Archangel before he ever earned his wings, literally ran away with the circus, though she never became a performer herself. Ellis once told Talbot that it was Martha who had first conceived of his Angelic persona and encouraged him to form his own act. Without this small, reserved woman, the Archangel would never have flown at all.

Talbot squatted down in front of the grieving widow, careful not to allow his heel to catch in the hem of his cassock. He covered both of her hands with his own and waited for her to make eye contact. "Martha, I'm so sorry for your loss. Ellis was my friend, and I loved him."

The widow drew in her breath and steeled herself to speak. "Thank you, Talbot. My husband was very fond of you, too. He said you were the only priest he ever met who still remembered you were a human being. The service was beautiful. No one could have done better."

Talbot thanked his friend's widow and started to rise, but she held onto his hands.

"My husband's wake is tonight at the Tipsy Clown. The children and I have something special planned, but I have to speak. Half the town will be there, and I am scared to death already. You will be there, too, won't you?"

He had heard that strain before in the voices of grieving family members. The public rituals of death were exhausting and at times needlessly taxing for the bereaved. Even so, the clergyman knew the hardest part was yet to come. After the funerals and wakes were over and the visiting mourners had gone back to their lives, Martha would be alone in a new silence. That was when the grieving would really begin.

"Of course, I will be there, Martha. And don't worry about speaking in front of everyone. I think you'll find these folks to be a gentle audience. I certainly have."

*****

Talbot lifted his stole over his head, hung it on the coat rack wedged into the corner of his office and began to unbutton his cassock. The church office was barely more than a large closet located behind the chancel area of the church. In fact, the only feature that distinguished the cramped space from a closet was a door that opened to the outside, that allowed parishioners to enter without having to walk through the sanctuary itself. Too small for a desk, the only furniture in the room was a pair of rocking chairs, a battered but serviceable bookshelf and the coatrack. Previously he had worked in larger and more luxurious offices, but Talbot found that he preferred this Spartan space to those previous accommodations. The office reminded him of a monastic cell free from all distractions where he could focus on his work. The benefit of the rocking chairs came as a surprise. Even the most agitated of parishioners could not help but be soothed by their gentle motion.

His robe still swayed on the hanger when there was a knock on the outer door. Talbot genuinely enjoyed most of his parishioners and was generally glad to see them, but leading worship left him mentally exhausted. He preferred to spend at least an hour alone after a service ended. Knowing that the wake would be equally taxing, the last thing he wanted to do was chat the afternoon away with a church member. Nearly two decades of practice helped to remove the look of irritation from his face as he moved to open the door.

Talbot expected a familiar face on the other side of the door, but the man who looked back at him was a stranger. Not only was he a stranger but he was clearly not from Gibbtown. The man's perfectly combed hair was as carefully tended as a PGA golf course and showed no signs of concession to the Florida humidity. Muscular biceps filled out the sleeves of his perfectly pressed blue polo shirt that was tucked into an equally well creased pair of khaki pants. Talbot's irritation doubled at the sight of him. Tourists did occasionally stop by to visit the church.

Though small and ordinary in some respects, Gibbtown United Methodist, like many of the town's residents, concealed hidden treasures. The pews were padded in a riot of colors, all hand-sewn from cloth used to make costumes. The altar table rested on the back of fully ordained circus elephant, and the pulpit, carved from the same dark oak, took the shape of a ringmaster, one arm raised toward his audience. Unique as those features were, it was the stained-glass window at the rear of the church that drew the most visitors. The scene was common enough, the feeding of the five thousand found in the Gospel of Matthew. Jesus and his disciples were depicted in the standard fashion, wearing robes and sandals, frozen in place as they distributed the miraculously multiplied loaves and fishes. It was the hungry crowd, seated at the feet of the Lord, that made the Gibbtown window unique. Rather than an anonymous crowd of onlookers, the entire circus was gathered around Jesus. Crowds and acrobats waited alongside a giant, the bearded lady, a lion tamer. Even the famous Lobster Boy with his claylike appendages was present next to a pair of Siamese twins joined at the hip. Under normal circumstances Talbot was willing to give a tour of the church, but this was not the time.

Before the stranger could speak, Talbot held up his hand, palm out in a gesture of refusal, and said, "I'm sorry sir, but the church is closed for tours right now. Perhaps you could come back tomorrow if you are still in town."

The department store mannequin of a man smiled and extended his hand, unfazed by the rejection. "I'm not here for a tour sir, though I have heard that the church here in Gibbtown is special. My name is Preston Weems. I'm an investigator with Florida Mutual Life Insurance Company. I'm here to speak with Reverend Talbot Jones. Do you know where I might find him?"

Talbot's irritation deepened further than he thought possible, and he allowed a scowl to creep onto his face. The only person he wanted to talk to less than a tourist at this moment was an insurance salesman.

"I'm Talbot Jones, but this really isn't a good time. Before you ask me about coming back later, I'm as insured as I need to be and not all interested in a new policy."

Still unfazed by the clergyman's brusque rebuff, the insurance man remained firmly planted in the doorway as he spoke.

"Reverend Jones, I'm so glad to have found you. I'm not here to sell you anything. In fact, I'm not an insurance agent all. I'm a policy investigator, as I said before, and I would like to talk to you about one of our clients, Mr. Ellis Teller."

The new information about Weems jarred Talbot out of his irritation but not enough for him to invite the stranger into his office. His only experience with an insurance investigator came from one the classic radio programs that Talbot preferred to television. The man in front of him was too polished and overly friendly to bear much resemblance to Johnny Dollar and was unlike to have "an action-packed expense account."

"I'm surprised you're not aware of this, but Mr. Teller is dead. In fact, I only just concluded his funeral service. He suffered an accident while training for his act and died instantly."

The investigator lowered his hand, the one concession he made to Talbot's unfriendly posture. "Florida Mutual is very much aware of Mr. Teller's tragic death. That is why I'm in Gibbtown. In situations like this, it is standard procedure to interview the friends and family of the deceased before payment is made on their policy. I only have a few questions that shouldn't take more than fifteen minutes of your time. The sooner I can dot all the I's and cross all the T's, the sooner we can provide Mr. Teller's family with the financial assistance he has secured for them."

Nothing in the investigator's demeanor suggested deception, but Talbot had been a student of human behavior for a long time. Knowledge of God's ways was only half of the requirement for a good pastor. The other half was a careful study of where the divine intersected with the behavior of God's children. Something in the way the investigator used words like procedure and standard remind Talbot of Christ's interactions with the Pharisees. Nothing could conceal ill intent as readily as the language of bureaucracy.

"I'm confused. What do you mean 'situations like these'?"

The investigator changed his posture for the first time since their conversation began. He leaned in closer to Talbot and lowered his voice as if unwanted ears lurked in the church yard.

"The circumstances of Mr. Teller's death were, you have to admit, unusual. It's not every day that a man falls to his death from a trapeze. We simply want to ensure that his death really was an accident and nothing more. That's why I'm here. To talk to those closest to Mr. Talbot and hopefully gain some insight into his state of mind at the time of the accident. I've already spoken to several people who knew him, and one of them mentioned that the two of you were close. And after all, who better than a man's pastor to help me get a better understanding of his emotional health."

Ellis had not killed himself. Talbot was certain of that. Preston Weems had skirted the word suicide with his talk of company policy and emotional health, but that is exactly what he meant. The circumstances of Ellis's death were unusual. The investigator was right about that. In Gibbtown the unusual was ordinary. The people here built their lives on the ability to be unusual, and for some of them it wasn't a choice. Talbot felt a sudden urge to shove the stranger down the short flight of concrete steps that led up to the outer door of the office.

"I'm afraid I really don't have time to talk right now, even for fifteen minutes. If this is absolutely necessary to secure the money you owe Mr. Teller's family, we will have to meet sometime tomorrow."

Weems retreated down the steps, smiling as if he was about to end a visit with an old friend. "That is no problem, Reverend. The company has authorized me to stay in town as long as I need in order to make a judgment on Mr. Teller's claim. Would a dinner meeting work for you, say 6:30 at the clown restaurant? It seems to be the only game in town for a sit-down meal."

"Here. Take my card in case you want to get in touch with me sooner."

Talbot took the offered card but didn't look at it. "The name of the restaurant is the Tipsy Clown, and the food is actually very good. As for the appointment, that sounds fine, but I will call you to confirm when I have had a chance to check my calendar."

"Thank you for the correction and for your time. I look forward to talking with you tomorrow."

Weems turned and started to walk toward a black Mercedes parked a few feet away but stopped after only a few steps. "I grew up in the Methodist church, you know. My parents are members of First UMC in

Tampa, not all that far from here. I wonder if you've ever crossed paths with either of them. They are both pretty involved in their congregation."

Talbot forced a note of cordiality into his voice when he replied. "I doubt it. There are a lot of Methodists in this part of Florida, and Gibbtown is a bit of a world unto itself."

"You're right about that. This town is practically another planet. You're right about there being a lot of Methodists, too. Still, it can't hurt to ask. Who knows, we might know each other better than we think."

*****

The sound of the Archangel's wake could be heard for several storefronts beyond the entrance to the Tipsy Clown. Downtown Gibbtown occupied less than a mile of street-front property. Most of the buildings were low brick structures built in the late forties and early fifties. Only the Clown defied the architectural inclination toward function over form. Two stories tall and clad in clapboard siding, the Tipsy Clown was a replica of the sort of hotel and salon that would have looked at home in Dodge City when the West was still wild. Not content to be merely archaic in design, the clown was painted in a rainbow of polka dots roughly four feet in diameter. A drunken patron who stepped into the street and gazed too long at the exterior of the building was likely to end up a dizzy heap in the gutter.

Though the bar normally encouraged tourists to frequent the establishment, today was an exception. The neon sign that pulsed with the movements of a circus clown that staggered while drinking from a foam-topped beer stein was dark. In case the unlit sign was not enough to discourage unwelcome guests, a hand letter signed that read "closed for private event" was taped to the double saloon doors. Though their livelihood depended on public performance, the circus folk guarded their private moments with a seriousness that would have been the envy of many a secret society. Talbot was still honored and humbled by the fact that that though he had never swung on a trapeze or faced down a tiger, the people of Gibbtown welcomed him into the backstage of their lives.

Inside, the bar was packed to capacity. Most of the performers stood in clusters drinking and laughing, except for the elderly who sat at tables or in booths. A Jimmy Buffet song played the jukebox in the corner. Talbot made his way to the bar slowly, stooped every few feet to receive words of appreciation and handshakes for his role in the funeral. When he finally reached the bar, he took a stool next to an elderly tattooed man whose inked skin had sagged with time into a colorful but indistinct Rorschach test.

"Welcome, Reverend. That was a fine send-off you gave the Angel. Your drinks are on me today."

Maxwell Studs, the man who stood behind the bar with a tall pitcher of beer for Talbot, would never have been hired for a position in the hospitality industry anywhere except Gibbtown. Born with a large cyst-like growth beneath his left eye that proved impossible to remove, Max joined a touring freak show as a teenager. The tumor had expanded over time, gradually deforming both his cheekbone and eye socket, until it appeared that a single large eye occupied the center of his face. Posters from Max's circus days decorated the walls of the clown that showed him in his various personas, "The Cyclops" and "The Melted Man."

Talbot wrapped his hand around the beer stein and settled himself onto the bar stool. Since his arrival in Gibbtown, he had made it a point to eat several meals a week at the Tipsy Clown. For a people who were naturally distrustful of outsiders, his willingness to have office hours on their turf had earned him almost as much goodwill as the burial of the elephant. The beer was dark and slightly bitter, the way Talbot liked it. It was obviously one of Max's home brews that he reserved for more discerning customers.

"Max, you have done it again. This is a perfect porter."

The bartender smiled, a movement that affected only half of his face, the rest frozen into a perpetual leer that exposed misaligned teeth. "I'm glad you like it. You're the first to taste my new recipe."

The Melted Man started to walk, ready to attend to other customers, but Talbot stopped him. "Max, I know you're busy, but I have question to ask you."

Max turned his full attention on Talbot, his head tilted slightly to give his good side a better angle. "I'm never too busy for the man who buries our dead. What's on your mind?"

"Did a man come here today asking questions about Teller or where he could find me? He looks to be in his mid-thirties, good tan, definitely from out of town."

Max looked down at an invisible spot on the bar and began to rub it with the bar towel that hung at his waist. The tension that could not show on his disfigured face was evident in the rapid motion of his arm and wrist.

"He sure did. Normally, I would have kept quiet if a townie who looked like that came in here asking about one of ours. He said he knew you from another church and that he had something important to talk to you about. With the funeral and all, I thought you might want to be found. Was that the wrong thing to do? If it was, I'm sure sorry, Preacher."

Talbot was touched by the fact that the bar owner considered him worthy of the secrecy that was normally only afforded to the locals themselves. He also wished that in this case it had actually been applied. Still, Max had not betrayed him deliberately.

"No Max, it's fine that you told him where to find me. I was just wondering where he got the information."

The bartender stopped wiping the spotless bar top but kept his good eye focused on Talbot. He leaned over the bar, his face inches from Talbot's.

"Is everything OK, Rev? You're not in trouble, are you?"

In another place Talbot was certain that the possibility of the pastor being in some sort of trouble would have been a source of gossip and scorn. He was equally sure that when Max asked the question, his intention was entirely different. What the Melted Man wanted to know was if Talbot needed to be hidden for a few days while a few of the more intimidating citizens gathered to encourage the stranger to leave town.

"I'm not in any trouble that I know of. In fact, that there probably isn't any trouble at all."

"You know, Preacher, if you ever were in trouble, you could come to me. Folks around here think highly of you, and we take care of our own."

"Thank you, Max. I appreciate that. I really do. I also hope I never have to ask for that sort of help."

Max grinned, a sight that would have inspired Bela Lugosi to new heights of horror, and slapped the bar.

"Isn't that the truth? Drink up, Rev. The Archangel was a good man, and he'll be missed."

Talbot hoisted his glass as Max shuffled to the other end of the bar, his attention already focused on another customer. The Archangel had been a good man, one of the best Talbot had ever known. For the first time, though, that troubled him. Ellis had given all of himself to the circus. He was on the road more than he was home, and when he was home, he was practicing or designing a new, ever more spectacular routine. Talbot knew he had performed with injuries but nothing that put his life at risk any more than it already was. For all of his devotion, Ellis never allowed his dedication to his art to cost his family. As often as he could, he took Mary and the twins on the road with him. He was awe inspiring as the Archangel, but Ellis Teller was an even better father.

Times had been tough for the performers in Gibbtown for more than a decade. The circus was changing, dying in some places and taking on new forms of life in others. Talbot had more than once thought that the circus and the church shared similar life cycles if not objectives. Both of Ellis's children would soon go away to college. Work had been slim for a long time, and Talbot knew that like so many others in Gibbtown, the

Archangel had struggled to make ends meet. How far would his friend have gone to provide for his family?

The dark turn of his thoughts was interrupted by a gentle hand on the small of his back and a whispered voice marked by a heavy Spanish accent in his ear.

"Would you like to dance, or would it be unseemly for the town priest to be seen cavorting with a circus performer?"

Talbot put his beer down but was careful to keep his eyes straight ahead. The voice and the touch caused him to shiver and betrayed any hope he might have had at appearing unaffected.

"I'm not a priest and therefore dancing with a beautiful woman is certainly allowed. As for unseemly cavorting, perhaps we could save that for later."

Talbot pivoted on the barstool and he wrapped his arms around the woman who whispered in his ear. The skintight sequined costume she wore at the funeral was gone, replaced by a simple black dress that displayed her muscular shoulders. Even seated, Talbot was able to look over the top of her head where her dark hair, pinned back for the performance on the coffin, now flowed freely past her shoulders. Silvia Loza, scion of the great Bolivian circus, carried herself with the grace of royalty, and Talbot loved her more than he believed possible.

"In that case follow me and try to restrain yourself."

Talbot did not say a word as he took her hand and followed her into the space in front of the jukebox reserved for dancers. Well attuned to public scrutiny, he felt eyes on them as they made their way onto the dance floor. Of all the miracles Talbot met with in Gibbtown, his relationship with Silvia and the town's response astonished him the most. There had been no gossip or murmurs of disapproval, in fact just the opposite. More than a few members of his congregation, the Archangel included, encouraged him.

Silvia pushed a button on the jukebox and brought forth the sound of a Latin guitar played low and mournful. The pair merged together, and after a few chords were joined by other dancers. Talbot rested his chin on the contortionist's head and closed his eyes. The music ached with every note, and yet beneath the tones of loss was a quick rhythm, a promise that even the most broken hearts could mend. Pressed against Silvia, they barely swayed in time to the music. For the first time that day, Talbot allowed his pastoral reserve to slip. Tears ran down his face and into her hair. Silvia tightened her arms around his waist and spoke softly in the hollow of his chest.

"You will miss him, won't you?"

Talbot's reply was barely a whisper. Any more, and his voice would have cracked with emotion. "Yes, I will. Ellis chose to be my friend before I gave him a reason to be. He took care of me when it was my job to take care of other people."

Talbot paused before he asked the question, afraid that if he spoke the words out loud, he would some- how speak a painful answer into being. "Do you think Ellis meant to fall, that his accident wasn't really an accident?"

Silvia's reaction was sudden, her arms extended to push him back, though she kept her hands on his hips. "Why would you ask me such a thing as that?"

Her response surprised him, and his face reddened, but Talbot's doubts forced him to continue. "A man from Ellis's insurance company came to see me today. Apparently, he had a very large policy to be paid out on the event of his death. The investigator seems to think Ellis might have fallen on purpose."

Her voice softened but her eyes locked firmly on Talbot's. "And what do you believe?"

Belief. Why did she have to use that word? Belief was more than knowledge or suspicion and encompassed more than facts, even superseded them at times. Talbot did not believe in much. What he did believe had kept him alive at times when the alternative would have been far easier. He also knew that belief was not a matter of wishful thinking or a need to hide from his fears. Life moved in ways that he did not always understand, but the current that moved his life was steady and trustworthy.

"I believe that Ellis was as good a man as I have ever known and that everything he ever did, he did because he believed it was right."

Silvia moved close and pressed herself back into his chest. As if she led a small child who was afraid of the dark, she began to sway in time to the music. "I believe that, too."

Before either of them could say more, their conversations were interrupted by a soft voice amplified by the bar's sound system. The Tipsy Clown offered live shows in an effort to attract tourists, and the bar was equipped with a small stage. The house lights dimmed, and all conversation stopped when a spotlight illuminated a single figure on the stage. The Archangel's widow, Martha Teller, stood in the light, still in her funeral dress, and held a microphone in her trembling hands.

"All of you know that I am not a performer. I have always left the spotlight to my husband. Tonight will not be any different. Before I give the stage back to him one last time, there is something I want all of you to know. My husband loved this town and he loved all of you."

The spotlight went dark, and the Archangel's widow was gone as quickly as she had appeared. For the space of a single breath the Tipsy Clown was silent before it erupted in thunderous applause, hoots and whistles. Teller never heard applause at the conclusion of a eulogy before but he understood why he heard them now and joined in himself. The people of Gibbtown gave all of themselves to their performances. They knew a herculean effort when they saw one. Martha Teller had pushed past her fear and grief to give them her best and they responded in the way they knew best.

The applause was still going full force when the stage curtain was pulled back to reveal a large screen. Off to one side, a pair of the Archangel's wings hung suspended by wires from the ceiling. The wings appeared so lifelike that if they had begun to beat of their own accord and flown out over the audience, the crowd would not have been surprised. The applause died completely when a projector mounted on the ceiling began to display a familiar scene for the gathered mourners.

The film began with a close-up of Ellis in his Archangel costume. He wore a skintight gold shirt printed to look like a soldier's breast plate, tights printed with golden shin guards and, of course, his wings. Jubilant music, heavy with the sound of blared trumpets played as Ellis took to the air. The camera panned away from Ellis to the circus tent where invisible projectors created the illusion of a star-filled sky streaked with the movement of other angelic figures.

Talbot recognized the performance immediately and choked back tears.

Ellis Teller had been a bright, intensely creative man, but the demands of circus life had stalled his formal education just shy of a high school diploma. Not long after they met, Talbot joked that a man who called himself the Archangel must be a Milton scholar as well as an acrobat. Ellis, without the slightest sign of embarrassment, confessed that he had no idea what his new pastor was talking about. Talbot immediately loaned him his own battered copy of *Paradise Lost,* only half expecting it to be read. The next night Talbot was awakened by a knock on the door of his box-filled parsonage. It was Ellis. He had read the entire epic poem in two days. The show Talbot and the others now watched was the performance inspired by the blind poet.

After a seemingly effortless series of twists and turns on the trapeze, the scene around the Archangel changed abruptly. The tent sky above the audience darkened, thunder rolled through the big top, and lightning flashed in time with pounding kettle drums. On the platform opposite the Archangel a figure appeared, clothed entirely in a skintight body suit that concealed even the creature's face. The audience below let out a collective gasp as Shadow and Archangel plunged toward one another. The sound from the audience increased when the two performers nearly collided. At the moment they appeared to make contact, the Shadow's suit illuminated from within to reveal shifting demonic features.

The battle continued for some time in a series of ever more complex maneuvers until the demon struck what appeared to be a fatal blow, and the Archangel fell. Talbot remembered this moment well. A woman somewhere in the audience screamed in actual terror, she was so convinced by the Archangel's crumpled fall. Just at the moment it appeared his death spiral was irretrievable, the Angel straightened his body and grasped an invisible trapeze bar suspended in the darkness.

The Archangel soared up, and the battle resumed. The next time the demon attacked, heaven's defender was ready. Ellis caught the demon by its outstretched arms and held it tight. The demon struggled, writhed as if it actually wanted to be dropped as its suit pulsed faster and faster in a shifting pattern of light. At the apex of their swing the Archangel released his captive into the air. The entire scene went dark until seconds later a ring of fire blazed to life. The demon fell through the ring, screamed as it went, and darkness fell again. When the lights came back, the projected angels returned to the heavens above the three rings of the circus, and Ellis stood on the highest trapeze platform, his wings unfolded in a sign of certain victory.

The video stopped abruptly after a close-up of Ellis Teller's face then went black. Without any fanfare the stage curtains closed, the sound of the electric motors that controlled them audible in the silence. Talbot looked down at Silvia where she was burrowed into his ribs. Silent tears trailed down her face. Ellis made perfection appear effortless. Every movement was perfectly timed. Even when he appeared to fall, pulled into darkness, he was in control. Death was only an illusion.

*****

The knock on the office door was strong and quick, assertive without being aggressive. Talbot took a deep breath and offered a prayer as he slowly exhaled. "Lord, make haste to help me."

When he opened the door, Preston Weems stopped on the other side, the same smile on his face that seemed to suggest the two men shared some off-color confidence. Like before, he wore perfectly pressed khaki slacks and polo shirt. This time the shirt was canary yellow, a color that accentuated his well-cultivated tan. In one swift motion the investigator removed a pair of mirrored aviator sunglasses with one hand and extended the other to Talbot.

"Good morning, Reverend. I was glad to get your call last night. Meeting earlier in the day always suits me better, but the offer of a meal still stands if you like."

After a brief handshake, Talbot stepped aside and allowed Weems to enter the church office. He took a seat in the rocking chair that faced the exterior door and gestured for the other man to take the chair opposite him.

"Please sit. To be perfectly honest, I haven't stopped thinking about your concerns regarding Ellis's death since we talked yesterday. It didn't feel right to wait any longer than necessary to give what you need to do your job."

Preston Weems eased into the rocking chair and looked around the cramped office. The wide eyes and downturned mouth reminded him of the time he encountered a homeless man who over the course of a meal shared that he had a Ph.D. in physics. Talbot remembered the feeling of shock and pity at seeing someone fallen so far. When the investigator's eyes came to rest on Talbot, the expression was gone replaced by the now familiar grin.

"I knew you would see it that way, Reverend Jones. I thought I recognized you yesterday, but it took me a while to remember where I had seen you before. You spoke at a youth rally at my church that I attended when I was in high school. That's been over a decade ago now, but I still remember parts of your sermon. You talked about the value of telling the truth even when it came at a cost. As soon as I remembered that, I knew you would help me out. We aren't like the people in this town. From what I can see, most of them are con men or women of one sort or another. Everything they do is some sort of scam."

Talbot understood now. No one else that Weems had spoken to had given him any reason to question the circumstances of Ellis Teller's death, if they had spoken to him it all. Talbot could see the shrugged shoulders and hostile looks that would have been directed at the investigator as clearly as if he had been there himself. Talbot was his only hope for a chink in the town's armor. Weems was sharp. Talbot had to give him that. Reminding him of the days before he came to Gibbtown and the fall from grace it implied was a brilliant tactic. It might have worked if Weems knew him better. Talbot had fallen from grace but not because he committed a crime or some grave sin. He had simply worked himself into exhaustion and a divorce. Though those were sins enough in Talbot's mind, they were not the sort the investigator was imagining. Moving to Gibbtown was a decision that saved him from a nervous breakdown or worse, and Talbot never regretted it.

"What is it exactly that you want to know, Mr. Weems?"

Weems leaned forward in the rocking chair and looked Talbot directly in the eye when he spoke.

"I know that people see insurance companies and especially guys like me as the enemy. I show up, and folks assume, pardon my language, that big money is here to screw the little guy. That simply isn't true. If anything, my job is to protect the little guy from people who want to take advantage of the system. If Florida Mutual paid out on every personal injury, faked house fire or accidental death that came down the pike, we wouldn't be able to help our honest clients. We would be out of business, and honest people who are just having a run of bad luck would have no one on their side. My company isn't here to finance people who make bad choices and put their lives on the skids. We are here to help good people who need a hand through tough times."

Talbot rocked forward and held Weems eyes with his own.

"Have you ever read the *Book of Job,* Mr. Weems?"

For the first time since the two men met, Weems seemed unsure of himself, stumbled as he answered the question.

"I'm sure I have somewhere along the way, but it's been awhile. Job was the guy who suffered so much, right? Why do you ask?"

"It just seems to me that a man in your line of work would want to know the *Book of Job*. Job was a good man, 'blameless before God,' as scripture puts it. He even prayed for his children in case they forgot to pray for themselves. When his life fell apart and he lost everything, even his health, he knew it wasn't his fault. Eventually, Job's friends showed up to offer the poor bastard their support, though I suspect they may have been there to gloat, too. Those friends of Job's talked an awful lot about the rules. They explained that only sinners and the wicked suffered. They made it clear to Job that if he was suffering, it was all his own fault. Each in his own way explained to Job that if he would just admit what he had done wrong, everything would go back to the way it was. Job wasn't having it. He stuck to his guns and told his buddies he could take their rules and stick them where the sun doesn't shine. As it turns out, they were all in for a surprise. God showed up and told Job's friends that the Almighty didn't care much for their rules, especially the ones that tried to turn the creator of the universe into a tamed house pet that had to do what they expected. Job was surprised, too. He got more of God than he bargained for, but it was his friends with all their rules about good and bad that had to eat crow."

Preston Weems leaned away from Talbot, his knuckles white on the arms of the rocking chair.

"Listen, pastor, I'm no Bible scholar and I'm not sure what all of that is supposed to mean, but there is something I do know. None of the people in this town have made an honest living in their lives. Hell, their stock in trade is tricks that pull the wool over the eyes of normal people. Ellis Teller may have dressed up like an angel but he wasn't one. He had debts, big ones, and I don't believe his death was an accident. If you're a man of God like you claim to be, don't you think you ought to tell me the truth instead of giving me the run around like all of these damn carnie freaks?"

Talbot leaned back in the chair and smiled. It wasn't the first time he had said something someone didn't want to hear and had his faith questioned for his trouble. Weems was right about one thing, though. He did have an obligation to the truth. The same sort of truth that Job found in the center of a holy hurricane. There was more to life than he would ever understand and to pretend otherwise was the worst lie of all. Sometimes all anyone has is belief.

"Mr. Weems, the truth is Ellis was a good man, no angel, but a good man is dead. If he paid your company to look after his family when he was gone, then that is exactly what you should do. Now, if you don't mind, I have important work to finish. As I'm sure you noticed, my office is quite small. You can show yourself to the door."

The Fisherman

One fish, one taut flash of life against his line was all Jason McCann needed. The mountain trout, current caught between rock and water, needed nothing. All instinct and dappled scales, they lived as pure presence in the constant beginning and never ending of the river. Jason was sure the trout sensed his desperation, like pain along flared nerve endings, broadcast along the hand-braided line. They sensed his un-belonging and turned away in search of less desperate prey. On another day, fish and fisherman would have been equals, pure existence above and below the rush of water. Not today. Today Jason was the father of a daughter and so the fisherman knew need.

"Shit."

The line pulled taut with promise. It took Jason only a split second to realize the pitch of his hope was wrong, the angle too steep and constant. A hooked trout would have pulled back to slacken the line then burst away in an effort to free itself. The fixed tension on the line meant only one thing. The carved tip of the rabbit-bone hook, hair-fine and fragile but blind, had found the wrong prey. If he pulled to free the hook, it would snap against the rock or another piece of stream debris that held it. Broken, the hook would be useless. It was the last of three, all carved from the remains of a meal eaten weeks ago. There was no time to make more. Ellie would arrive in a few hours. Not that more time would have mattered. His snares were empty, had been for days, and the raw material for the hooks was absent.

Jason knelt down and anchored the tight line beneath a stone on the stream bank. With the line secured against the pull of the current, he began to undress. It was early November on the mountain. Jason had begun to think of the entire landscape as his, though not in the way of deeds or property lines. The mountain fed him, sheltered him, saved him, and he loved it in the way a dependent child loves a reliable parent. The mountain could be harsh and unforgiving at times, but it was never absent. Full winter was still weeks away, but altitude made the nights and early mornings January cold. Jason wore almost every article of clothing he owned, layered to salvage the heat from his body.

He removed the short cape first. It was made from the ancient skin of a coyote killed before Jason was born. The hide hung on the wall of the cabin Jason had called home for decades until he took it down from its resting place. The first time he wrapped the skin around his shoulders, felt the dust-laden tail brush his back, Jason felt foolish. He was a grown man wearing animal skin when less than ten miles away there were other human beings dressed in clothing engineered in a laboratory. Next, he took of the wool tunic and pants, both dyed an uneven green that ranged from forest to olive. Last were the nylon long-johns, hiking socks, and leather sandals that tied around his calves. Jason felt his flesh rise in a futile effort to extend his hair follicles evolved long past the ability to protect his bare skin. The long underwear and hiking socks were the only part of Jason's gear he had not made himself. All that remained was the pointed hood made from the same wool as the pants and overskirt. If he found himself deep enough in the stream to soak the hood, he would have more serious concerns to deal with.

"This is going to hurt."

Left to himself Jason would have tugged on the line and hoped for the best. There was still plenty of food to forage even without the yield from traps or hooks. He had gone for weeks on a diet of edible plants that could be harvested with almost no effort. Food gathered from the forest floor would not be enough for Ellie. If his daughter returned from the visit and complained to her mother of hunger, his daughter's already infrequent visits would stop altogether.

Naked except for the pointed wool cap, Jason bent down to retrieve his line from underneath the rock. He looked at the water and followed the slender brown thread to the point where it submerged at midstream. He was grateful the water was too turbulent to provide even a hint of his reflection. Undressed, except for the pointed wool cap, Jason was certain he looked like an oversized garden gnome at a nudist colony. He tried to avoid moments that made him feel like a ridiculous child trying to escape from the responsibilities of a grown man. Liz, Ellie's mother, certainly felt he was.

"Jason, you can't do this. We have a daughter."

"I'm doing this for her, for all of us. I want to have a real life away from all of this bullshit."

"How is living in a hut on the side of a mountain a real life?"

"Liz, I just can't do this anymore."

"Neither can I."

There had been other arguments, screaming, and tears. All of it had fused into one agony that left Jason afraid and full of doubt when he replayed those moments in his mind. Survival in the mountains with only a few primitive tools required constant effort.

During the day as he gathered food, checked his snares, or collected firewood there was little time to think. The nights were different. In the dark he remembered in endless loops until he fell asleep. He thought mostly of Ellie and wondered if his daughter missed him.

Jason stepped into the stream and felt one foot then the other burn and go numb from the cold. The water was shallow, waist deep at the center, but the current was strong and the rocks were slick. It would be easy to fall and hit his head on a rock. He wondered if he could drown and not know it.

He and Liz were never married. They met on a nature hike he led when he still worked for the Forest Service. Three months later Liz told him she was pregnant. They moved into a rented shotgun house in a former mill village turned hipster enclave two weeks before Ellie was born. Their neighbors kept chickens in the backyard and planted organic kale instead of flowers in the front. Jason was happy. For what felt like a long time, he was happy.

The pain was quick and sent electric jolts of adrenaline through his groin. Jason resisted the urge to jerk his foot back and risk a fall. One misstep, and he was now wedged between two water black river stones. A gentle push on one rock, and he was free. He would have to warm up before he could tell if his ankle was sprained or not. For now, it didn't matter.

Things had changed when the government shut down. Jason never cared much about politics outside of a general concern for conservation issues. When he was told that all the Forest Service employees would be out of work until the politicians in Washington could reach an agreement over the budget, he was excited. Liz made good money as a nurse and a week of unpaid vacation was still vacation.

He enjoyed the first two weeks. Liz went to work, and Ellie was dropped off at day care. Alone in their small house, Jason read the survival manuals and built a boat he constructed according to a millennia-old Cherokee design. He prepared meals from a frontier cookbook he found at a small branch library a few blocks from the house.

"Jason, that smells delicious. What is it?"

"The book calls it iron kettle stew. The recipe is really old."

"Are we going to be pioneers now?"

"Would that be so bad? We could make and grow everything we need. Ellie would not have to go to day care anymore. We can be together."

"I think I would miss indoor plumbing."

Jason leaned into a large rock that broke the current midstream. He flinched when the cold stone made contact with his bare flesh. He wound the cord twice more around the palm of his hand to remove some but not all the slack in the line. From where he stood Jason could see a partially submerged log wedged against the stream bed. His line disappeared beneath it, the hook likely snagged in sodden wood. He would have to kneel in the cold water up to his chest and hope he found the slender hook before his fingers went numb.

They had stayed in the old cabin before. Backed up against the national forest and accessible only by four-wheel-drive, the old shack once belonged to Jason's grandfather. There was no possibility the cabin would ever have electricity or running water.

"We could live here if we wanted to. We'd have everything we need."

"No, we don't. This is fun for the weekend, but this place is not home. There are no lights. Ellie can't take a bath."

"I can take care of you here, I know I could. Liz, I can't go back."

Jason stepped away from the shelter of the boulder and stumbled into water over his waist. With the violent contraction of his body, the cold water stopped him from breathing, but he knew better than to stop. He braced himself against the algae-slick log and knelt down in the stream. He ran his hand down the line until it passed under the fallen tree. His fingers brushed something smooth, and the line pulled against his palm. Jason pulled back and rose out of the water.

The trout was perfect. Two pounds at least. It had swallowed the bone hook completely, and the tip protruded from the gills on one side of the fish's head. Wounded, it had dived under the log to escape and became trapped. Jason held it by the lip and watched the fish twist a few times then give up. The uninjured gill still pulsed slowly. Bright pink stripes ran the length of its silver green body, exactly the color of the parka Ellie wore when she came to visit. Jason wondered if she would notice the color when they cleaned the fish before they cooked it. If not, he would show her.

Dappled Things

Fleck thought the girl was dead. Most of her body was covered by a small sailboat that had been overturned and raised on a pair of sawhorses for the hull to be scraped. One pale arm extended out from the shadowed sanctuary, already pink from the sun. Could a dead body sunburn? Fleck wasn't sure, but he didn't think so.

He crouched down and squinted in the darkness under the boat. His calves tightened, ready to spring back like a hunter who has run a wounded animal to ground. The cloistered shadows of the hull made it difficult for him to see, forced him to press his face into the ship-turned cell. Her face was turned from him, buried in the bend her other arm. Fleck listened for breathing, but all he could hear were gull cries over the marsh and the thick pop of tide water against pluff mud. He pulled his face back and looked down at the arm. It was perfectly still and less than an inch from his foot. Fleck had touched the dead bodies of animals, but never a human being.

He pressed one tentative finger into the flesh just above the girl's wrist. The skin was warm, blossomed white, then back to sunburned rose. She was alive. Relieved of the burden of finding a dead body, Fleck shifted into more familiar territory. He could a help a living stranger in trouble. He grabbed the woman's wrist, this time in a firm grasp and shook it.

"Ma'am are you all right? Are you OK?"

His voiced echoed, louder than he expected off the dome of the capsized boat. Fleck felt the wrist pull from his grasp as the prone figure rose quickly. Her head struck a board that served as a bench in the small vessel and fell back onto her arm. He was about to repeat his question when the woman spoke, head still turned away from him.

"I don't want any trouble. I just needed some place to crash. Give me a minute, and I'll be out of here. Just don't call the cops. Please." Most of the words were muffled, half lost in a groan, but the last was clear.

"I wasn't going to call the police. I just wanted to make sure you were all right. You weren't moving…"

Fleck allowed his explanation to trail off unfinished. Instinct suggested that it was impolite to reveal to a living woman that he suspected her of being a corpse. Fleck possessed a hard-earned gift for sensing fragile dignity and treating it with care.

"I'm fine, but I'd like to get out from under this boat now. I've slept in worse places but I think I'm done with this one."

He stood up and stepped back, aware now that he blocked her exit from the improvised shelter. Fleck turned away as she slid out from the dry-docked boat. Gravel rasped as she pulled free. He considered turning around to help her but decided against it. Hands slapped against clothing, Fleck supposed, to remove a layer of dust before she spoke.

"You can turn around now. I'm not naked."

Fleck felt the sting of blood that rushed up his neck and over his scalp. He had turned away to spare the stranger the indignity of being watched as she wriggled in the dirt, but that was not the only reason for the display of modesty. Thirty-two years of familiar eyes made him accustomed to regular scrutiny. No matter how much time passed, the reaction of strangers who saw his face for the first time was painful. Most stared briefly then shifted their eyes, pretended not to notice. Others remained uncomfortable, looked away then back again, unable to help themselves. Whatever the response, he was reminded of a distance that could not be crossed.

Fleck turned around, careful to keep his head up. As much as he hated this moment, he had learned that any sign of shame on his part only made it worse. She was small, her head not quite the level of his chest. Slender arms and a collar bone visible through her thin T-shirt reminded Fleck of dolls woven from dried palmetto leaves; brittle and fragile. Her blonde hair was cut in a ragged line that reached her chin and, pushed back, revealed a line of metal studs that formed a ladder up her left ear.

"Hold it loose, or it will crush," the weaver women in the market often said when they placed a palm frond doll in the hands of a tourist's child. "Be careful, and that doll will make it home with you."

"That's beautiful. Did it hurt?"

Fleck was too surprised to even flinch. The girl's fingers brushed his forehead, over the bridge of his nose, jaw, and down his neck. Her touch, so light her fingers seemed to hover over his skin, followed the line of his birthmark.

"They're so small. It must have taken forever to do that. Did you design it yourself?"

Fleck's head swam and his eyes lost focus. Sunlight separated into bands of color that refused to assemble into a unified white. The strawberry dots that formed a broad band across his face seemed to quiver against one another like atoms pushed to split. Fleck spoke, but his voice sounded hollow, disembodied.

"What?"

The single word spoken in no particular direction and without clear intent fractured the moment, stalled creation before it could begin. The girl drew her hand back into her chest. She cradled it like the owner of small dog, stopped before it could bite an unprepared stranger.

"Oh, God. I'm so sorry. I do that sometimes; forget about other people's space. It's just that I've never seen ink like that before. I should have asked before I touched it. I'm really sorry." Absent her hand on his face, Fleck's vision returned. The bands of violet, amber, and green merged together into coherent objects; the girl, the boat, swaying marsh grass. Though he could see, speech remained a mystery. Words seemed broken, as if he was made to translate between languages, grasped for phrases he understood to make sense of the whole. He seized a single word and spoke it aloud, a clue to meaning.

"Ink?"

The girl looked up from her chastened hand. Her confused expression mirrored Fleck's own.

"Your tattoo, all those patterns. They're like the dots in a comic that make the picture. It's beautiful."

She meant his birthmark. The realization dawned on him like the discovery of a lost letter to an undecipherable alphabet. The girl thought he had done this to himself and admired him for it. Expectation and history so utterly displaced left him without direction, unsure how to continue. Fleck raised his hand to his face and followed the track of her ghost fingers. He laughed.

"What's so funny?"

He had made her angry. Her tone was so familiar Fleck could read the contours of her life in those few words. She thought he was laughing at her, one more in a long line of others who had done the same. Fleck knew what to do.

"I'm not laughing at you. I'm just surprised. No one has ever thought I did this to myself before. It's not a tattoo. It's a birthmark. I was born like this."

"Are you serious? It's just so perfect."

Fleck fought the urge to laugh again when she stepped closer, her head tilted back to allow her eyes to scan his face. Her body was so near to his, Fleck only had to bend his arm at the elbow to extend his hand.

"I'm Fleck."

The girl looked down at his paint-stained hand before she pressed her palm against his. Fleck remembered the advice of the old woman at the market and kept his hand loose, a place to rest not to be held.

"My name is Amy."

******

"They're beautiful."

Fleck watched as she picked up one of his carvings, a wood duck with a swept back mane of green feathers, and turned it over in her hands. The duck was new, finished just two days ago. As always when he worked, Fleck had lost all track of time and the world outside his workshop. The grain of the wood pulled him along until the bird took shape, refused to release him until it was free. He never knew what would emerge, a mallard, a teal, or some other water bird when he began. Fleck released himself to instinct and expectant trust when he took up his tools. So far they had never failed him.

"Thanks. I carved them all myself."

Amy placed the duck back onto his workbench. She picked up another, an unfinished marsh hen, before she spoke.

"What are they for?"

Another question that surprised him. Most people did not recognize the utility of his carvings even in an oblique fashion, assuming they were art for art's sake.

"They're hunting decoys, but people don't use them that way anymore. Most hunters now use plastic decoys that are cheaper and lighter."

"If no one uses them, why do you make them?"

"There are people who collect them as art, I guess. Mostly, I make them because I enjoy it and I can work alone."

Fleck paused, considered saying more. The truth was the hand-carved decoys made him more than a comfortable living. He shipped his work all over the world. Why would he want to tell her that? Nothing about this day or Amy made any sense. He invited her to his home on what at first seemed like an impulse. Now as he watched her wander through his shop, her hands trailing over his carving the way her fingers had touched his face, he realized impulse was wrong. Amy stirred some deep law that had to be obeyed but whose presence was previously unknown and therefore startling, difficult to trust. Her response was equally unexpected. She had agreed to come with him. She only hesitated long enough to retrieve a faded army surplus backpack from under the boat, as if invitation from a strange man was a daily occurrence. If that were true, Fleck considered that he might have made a mistake.

"Are you hungry?"

The question should have been an easy one. Amy put down the unfinished carving she held. Only a beak and the gentle inner curve of a neck of what he believed would be a mallard had emerged from the raw block of wood. Amy wiped her palm over the back of her other hand several times before she replied.

"Yes. It's been a while since I last ate."

The sensation of an unacknowledged but fundamental language barrier persisted for Fleck. Amy had followed him to his home, completely at ease, but the thought of sharing a meal appeared to make her anxious. Fleck felt as if they were speaking different dialects, shared words that held different meanings.

"Follow me. The kitchen is this way."

The walk from the shop to his home was a short one. The two structures were identical from the outside; longer than they were wide and made from red clay brick. After more than a century of South Carolina sun, salt, and wind, the brick had faded to a mottled and pitted orange. Both were former slaves' quarters, built from what remained after the main house was constructed. The plantation house was gone, burned down, and the land sold to make room for condominiums. Fleck occupied the remains of family legacy, a fingertip of live oak shaded land that pointed east over the estuary, past Folly Island to the Atlantic.

Fleck's home was simple, bordered on sparse. What furniture there was he carved for himself. The only adornment of any kind was a number of paintings in various sizes on the walls or permanently at rest on easels. He watched Amy move methodically through the house in silence. Deliberate but not tentative, her gentle drift though his home opened Fleck to a sort of life it had never occurred to him to imagine. His life was as routine as the rise and fall of marsh tides and as bounded. Anything else unsettled him. Amy was different. She seemed at home in newness and uncertainty.

"I don't have much to eat here. It's just me when I cook. Is an omelet ok?"

She turned from the painting she was staring at, an abstract sunset with violet rays that stretched to the edges of the canvas, and looked at him. The hesitation was back, the same stroking of her hands as before.

"Sure, but cheese OK. Don't put anything that makes noise."

"That's fine, but what do you mean 'makes noise'?"

The movement of her hands slowed but the pressure she exerted increased. Waves of pressed skin rolled in front of the edge of her palm.

"Sometimes when I eat, the sound is so loud it hurts. Soft food helps, but not all the time."

Fleck knew the moment well from his carving. Each piece was different, wanted to be known but gently. Nothing could be forced, or the work would be ruined.

"It doesn't get much softer than eggs."

******

"Why do they call you Fleck?"

It was the first real question Amy asked him. Over the course of the meal and throughout the course of the day, he had extracted her story, tentatively at first then with more assurance. Fleck knew she was from Ohio but had drifted from place to place most of her life; San Francisco, Portland, then back east, Nashville and Atlanta. Charleston was going to be her next stop, but she ran out of gas and money looking for the beach. When he asked why she never stayed anywhere, she had simply said, "Because nobody wants me to." As much as he wanted to give a real answer, Fleck faltered for the first time since he found her under the boat. He pointed to his face, tried to laugh and failed.

Amy was quiet. She rested her head on bent knees and stared out over the marsh. A flight of brown pelicans whispered low the water, enjoyed the only elegance in an otherwise ungainly life. The girl next to him was like these birds, an in-between creature. On the wing or when they plunged into the water with surgical precision, the pelicans were graceful, perfect. On land they were awkward, all odd angles and dislocation. When she forgot herself, Amy laughed easily, held nothing back. If she felt misunderstood or laughed at, she retreated, hid within herself. Fleck tried again.

"I guess you could say I named myself."

She kept eyes on the water, wary, when she spoke. "Why would you name yourself Fleck? It sounds like a dog's name."

"I didn't mean to. When I started school, some of the kids teased me. The called me stain or spot. I came home crying and told my momma. She told me my mark wasn't a spot or a stain. She said lots of babies were born with birthmarks, but they were smaller than mine and most faded away. Mamma said the marks were made by angels who carried babies to families who would love them. She said the angel who brought me to her must have loved me, too, because it wrapped me so tight in in its wings it left these little flecks all over me. When the kids at school started to tease me again, I yelled back, told them I wasn't stained that these were angel flecks. They thought that was even funnier, and the name stuck. I never told mamma that, but I imagine she figured it out later. Folks were bound to call me something. Better Fleck than spot or stain."

Amy lifted her head from her knees and looked at him. "You're lucky to have a mother like that." She paused before she spoke again but kept her eyes on Fleck. "Do you really have flecks all over you?"

"Yes."

"Will you let me see?"

"Yes."

*****

The sound was low and guttural, a mixture of fear and aggression. More asleep than awake, Fleck pushed the noise toward something familiar, raccoons slipped from the marsh, prepared to wage war for his trash can. The sound pitched up to a wail, sharp enough to tip the balance toward waking, then faded. Fleck reached for Amy to see if she had woken, too.

It was the first time he could remember not being ashamed of his dappled body. She had run both hands over the bruised purple marks, followed the unbroken ribbon down his face, over his chest, around his back and hip all the way to his right calf, where it stopped. Afterward they lay together, and she studied him, told him what she saw in the apparently random blotches like a sea captain with a star chart. Fleck's hand found nothing but an empty bed.

Fully awake, Fleck listened to the broken rhythm that woke him. It came from inside the house. Under the current of groans were words, audible but unintelligible. Fleck felt the fragile contentment that lulled him to sleep snap apart like a soap bubble in the hand of a child; easily made and more easily broken. He left the bed and walked through his darkened house.

Amy sat on the floor, naked, head between her knees. He watched her bare feet arch, heels lifted from the floor, then back down. The motion, repeated again and again, caused her body to tip and rest, like a warning channel marker. Fleck flinched when she groaned again. The space between his hips turned liquid and scalding.

He walked to where Amy sat, careful to soften his steps. Fleck sat down next to her, folded his body into a mirror of her own. She did not acknowledge his presence, but the low moan gave way to silence and the rocking stopped. Fleck started to speak but stopped himself. As much as he wanted to understand what was happening, he sensed that another voice was not what was needed. He stayed next to her until his body began to ache. Exhausted and stiff, he slipped quickly back to the bedroom, stripped sheets and a blanket from the bed and returned to Amy's side.

He draped the sheet over her shoulders and around her legs. Once the comforting shroud was in place, he folded the heavier blanket into a pallet for himself. He wanted to stay awake, to keep vigil until whatever darkness gripped her passed, but he was spent. The day had brought more than his solitary existence could contain, and his dappled flesh demanded rest. He stretched out almost close enough to touch Amy, rested his head on one folded arm and slept.

*****

Fleck kept his eyes shut and willed himself to stillness though the presence of sunlight called him to wake. He gave himself time to come fully awake before he risked looking to the spot where Amy should have been. The sheet he wrapped her in the night before was there, crumpled on the floor next to him, empty. Fleck sighed, rolled onto his back and pulled the sheet to him.

"You're awake."

Sore muscles pulled as Fleck sat up, the empty sheet cradled in his lap. Amy stood in the kitchen dressed in one of his paint spattered work shirts. She looked at him, met his eyes, but remained perfectly still.

"I was hungry, so I made eggs, but too many. Do you want some?"

Fleck felt the constellations of his starred flesh move, draw in and coil, prepared to push out, spread and create. A word was all that was required to put them in motion, after the long night of watching. He drew in the needed breath, felt it dance through mystery wrapped in his skin, and set it forth.

"Yes."

The Day of the Serpent

She flew up the mountain, fast, and wanted faster. Lettie almost missed the road sign that pointed to Titan Mountain. Even in daylight the barely marked break in the miles of concrete barrier was easy to miss. It was a miracle she had not white-knuckled on, deeper into the cleft of night highway and stone. This was the time for a miracle, past the time when miracles could have saved her, before half her time was pierced by pain. There had been so few signs for her lately, or at least none that she could see. Lettie kept one trembling hand on the steering wheel and stroked the purple bruise sealed in the flesh of her jaw. Providence and punishment were tangled, twisted beyond her comprehension.

She pressed down on the brake with swift but even force. The red Firebird was long past its prime, but the wide tires gripped the road, held the turn lane. Lettie had never driven the car, only sat in the passenger seat or turned the ignition as an act of memorial maintenance. She imagined the stencil winged phoenix spread in peeling white over the hood as a living thing, a once-proud protector softened by years but sharpened by guile. Lettie needed the old bird's winking vengeance to shelter her.

She turned and looked into the shadows of the cramped rear seats before she crossed the highway. Her daughter slept under a pile of quilts, body bent over the rise of the drive shaft. The Firebird was built for two. The shallow passenger seats seemed like more of an afterthought or an accident rather than a matter of deliberate design. Only the pliable body of an exhausted child or the desperate bodies of two seventeen-year-olds could find any comfort there. Lettie almost smiled. It was possible that the child slept, unaware of the danger that stalked them, in the very spot where she began.

Away from the highway the road narrowed, gave up even the pretense of a shoulder. Lettie tensed, then forced herself to take several deep breaths and slow the car to a painful crawl. She wanted to fly, push the car into the curves, and ride the center line the way Tommy had done. He was fearless in the Firebird, laughed and gunned the engine when she gasped and dug her fingertips into his thigh. Lettie was afraid. Tommy was gone.

Tommy would have been proud of her, touched the back of her neck and said, "That's my girl." The gravel path was impossible to see, but she felt it ahead and drifted off the paved road. The grade was steep, cut and carved by men who lived by the law of four-wheel drive. The bottom of the low sports car scraped over water-worn ruts, like the edge of a knife over a whetstone. Lettie winced at the sound and pulled her shoulders in, as if by contracting her own body, she could draw the car in with her. She drove on, grateful that her daughter still slept. After an eternity of branches shrieking over paint and slipped tires on loose rock, the road leveled out and stopped on a flat space on the mountain.

She ran her hands over the dashboard and gave thanks to the old warrior bird before she turned off the ignition. The darkness outside was absolute, and she waited for her eyes to adjust. The cabin had been in Tommy's family for generations. There had been talk of selling the old place and the parcel of rocky farmstead nearby. The web of ownership was so tangled, the effort was abandoned and the corner of mountain top remained a communal property. Too poor to afford anything else, she and Tommy spent their honeymoon in the cabin. Lettie had never been happier except for the day her daughter was born just shy of six months later. She wondered now if the memories worn into the boards and stone would shelter her or if the sanctuary would sense her sin and pass judgment.

Lettie pushed the car's heavy door open, twisted her hips, and slid out of the driver's seat. The full moon was visible through the thick canopy of oak and maple. It watched her with passive silver-slung serenity. The moonlight reminded her of the parachutists' wings Tommy had worn on his army uniform. The wings along with the carefully folded flag from his casket rested in a cardboard box in the Firebird's small trunk next to a bag of hastily purchased groceries. She wanted to take more, part of her certain that there would not be an opportunity to salvage more of her past, but there was no time. She had to run, take only what she needed most. The wings, the flag, the aging car and the little girl in the backseat would have to be enough. Tommy was gone, but the little girl had his eyes.

A few tentative steps in the darkness, and Lettie was up the stairs and through the unlocked door of the cabin. She wanted to make a place for her daughter to sleep before she brought her inside but she also did not want her to wake up alone in the dark. A camp lantern hung on peg inside the door. Lettie took it down and reached inside the pocket of her jeans for the lighter she had only recently begun to keep there. She primed the pump on the lantern's base and pressed the lighter at an awkward angle inside the glass globe. The flame was beginning to burn her fingers when the twin globes of the camp lantern bloomed to life. The bulbs looked like ripe muscadines lit from within like the faces of angels in a child's Bible.

The cabin smelled of dust and seeping damp that came with frequent mountain rainstorms. Built for shelter rather than convenience, there was no electricity, and unheated water flowed into a salvaged basin from a gravity-fed cistern higher up the slope. Generations of Tommy's family had made small additions and improvements to the cabin over the years. A simple kitchen area with shelves and a small propane stove to prepare meals had been installed in place of the massive cast iron cook pot that still hung in the stone fireplace. Before their wedding, Tommy had slipped away and built a shower stall with a wooded floor where a series of suspended reservoirs warmed in the sun.

Lettie pulled a pair of old camp cots away from the wall and brushed off a layer of dust, insect bodies and mouse droppings. In spite of her hurry, she lifted the corners of the worn mattress to check for spiders. The last thing she needed was for her daughter to be bitten by a black widow while she slept. Certain the bed was safe, she hurried out of the cabin and back to the car. The little girl had not stirred under her shroud of quilts. The deep angle of the Firebird's backseat was difficult, but she managed to lift the bundle of child and blankets and carry them inside. Lettie placed the girl on the cot and turned to extinguish the lantern when her daughter spoke for the first time since she fell asleep hours ago.

"Mama, are we in Daddy's special tree house?"

Her daughter had not moved, her head still covered by the folds of faded blanket, but she knew from experience that her eyes were wide open in the darkness. Lettie wanted to go outside, smoke a cigarette and breathe clouds of fear into the night. If she did, the child would wake, follow her outside, and neither of them would sleep for hours. Lettie walked over to the cot, slipped off her shoes, and squeezed onto the narrow mattress. She wrapped one arm over the bundle of blankets and pulled her legs up, made a new womb. Lettie pressed her mouth against the gentle rise of covered head, the pressure painful against her still swollen lip and lullaby whispered. "Yes, Stella. We are in Daddy's special tree house. You go back to sleep now. Mommy will be right here."

"I love you Mama."

"I love you too, Little Star."

******

It was hard to breathe inside the small cinder block church. Even with all the windows open and ceiling fans turning overhead, the air pressed down on the gathered congregation. The only movement came from the front the church.

"Sin is in us all, and we are all in sin. Every one of you rode the red whore of Babylon into this world. None of us are clean. There is only one thing that can make a sinner clean. One thing redder than that whore. Blood. Blood is the thing. The blood of Jesus."

Tyson Lindt slammed his open palm onto the worn wood of the pulpit and stretched Jesus into a lingering hiss. He learned both the pounded palm and the calculated "Jesus" whisper from a prison evangelist. Inmates were a tough audience. Most only attended worship services to prove their desire to reform to the parole board. So few of them believed in the blood. Tyson believed. He knew blood was power. The old evangelist knew blood too, knew how to make sinners want it more than drugs or sex. Tyson had listened and learned as the old man-made grown men, some of them killers, weep for the blood of Jesus with only the power of his voice.

He paused, scanned the congregation and ran a hand over his shorn skull. Sweat slid down and pooled into wet crystal scale, then rolled down his neck and under the collar of his starched white shirt. Tyson knew he was losing them. He had been preaching for more than twenty minutes, and the sermon was nearing conclusion. He needed them to lean forward hands in the air, call out "amen" and "yes, Lord" to fuel the altar call. Instead, most slumped in their pews, wilted by the heat inside the cinder block church, or stared out the window and waited for relief.

Tyson tapped the pulpit with his palms, stomped gently on the linoleum floor, built momentum for the final push. A low hum from the front pew, the sort animals make before a fight or bearing down with fangs to mate, drew his attention. Helen sat rigid against the hard back of the pew. Her head was angled, chin out, her exposed throat ringed by sweat. Hands folded she pressed thick fingers into the floral print of her dress, just below a spray of roses that covered the swell of her stomach. To the congregation the preacher's wife appeared lost in the Spirit moved by her husband's gift of the Word. Tyson knew better.

"Only blood will save us. Only blood will free us from Babylon's whore. Only blood will give us victory. Stand with me now and sing 'Victory in Jesus' and 'Remember the Blood.'"

In the corner the elderly pianist, blind in one eye, hesitated, then began to pound out the familiar hymn, the notes blurred by arthritic fingers. The congregation stood, surprise and relief obvious on some of their faces.

Tyson stepped down from the pulpit, closed his eyes, and leaned into the song. He should have gone on, stomped and shouted until they woke up or gave in to the Spirit out of sheer exhaustion. He might have if not for the promise of Helen's bare throat. Sickness and fear tingled at the back of his knees and withered his groin. Babylon had come for him, broken his will. Today he would triumph. Today he would be the sword of his own redemption.

*****

Birdsong, high and sweet-whistle-whispered Lettie awake. Eyes still closed, she could imagine the little wren had flashed through the trees and landed on legs less substantial than a shadow. The night was over, and the dawn bird was free to sing. Lettie's stomach twisted tight like a wrung dishrag, then melted into hot liquid. The contents of her stomach burned and pushed up her throat. She rolled off the cot and stumbled to the cabin door, one hand over clenched lips. Outside, she bent over the porch rail and felt the bark of the rough-hewn log bite into her skin through her thin T-shirt. The morning sickness was over quickly, disappeared into the moss and moist earth at the bottom of the staircase. She was still bent over the rail to give the cool air time to soothe her stomach when the cabin door opened.

"Mamma, are you sick?"

Stella stood in the doorway with the quilt pulled tight around her narrow shoulders. Her blonde hair was snarled from the rough night's shallow rest and a faint stain of dried spit marked the corner of her mouth and chin. There was no trace of sleep in her round blue eyes. Stella was a little girl but she was only rarely a child. She and Lettie had been alone all her life. They took care of each other. The sound of her mother throwing up had roused Stella as quickly as the same sound would have awakened the sleeping parent of a small child.

"No, baby, I'm fine. Something I ate must have disagreed with me. Do you want breakfast?"

"Sure Mamma. How do we cook here?"

"No cooking this morning, baby. There are pop tarts in the car along with some other groceries. You go back inside, and I'll bring them up."

Stella clapped her hands and caused the quilt to fall in a pile around her bare feet. "Did you get the strawberry kind with sprinkles on top?"

Lettie smiled and ran her hand from hip to hip over her stomach. She and Stella never had much, and Lettie was often surprised and a little ashamed of her daughter's gift for simple joy. "Why in the world would I buy those?"

"Mamma, you know the sprinkle kind are my favorite. Did you get them?"

"Yes, Stella, I got the sprinkle kind. Now pick up that blanket before it gets dirty. Daddy's tree house has just about everything we need except an easy way to wash our clothes."

The little girl scooped up the blanket and ran back inside, squealing "thank you" as she went. She couldn't hide her forever. Lettie knew that. She lied to her boss at the True Value Hardware store where she worked; told him she needed a week to take care of sick aunt just over the mountain in Tennessee. Lettie had worked at the store for a long time and always took extra shifts when the other employees wanted time off or called in sick. Mr. Pritchard said she was his most dependable employee and to take all the time she needed. Lettie tried not to look too shaken or cry when he pulled a hundred dollar bill out of his wallet and pressed it into her hand. Eventually, she would have to go back to work or lose her job, and Stella would start second grade in the fall. At least for now they were safe and she could figure out what to do next.

*****

"Stella, slow down and stay where I can see you." The little girl stopped, turned, waved, and ran up the trail, fueled by sugar and the excitement of a new place. It pleased Lettie to see her daughter so happy, and childlike. At home Stella would help to clean or fold laundry before she allowed herself to play. Lettie never asked for help. Stella seemed born with a sense of her mother's exhaustion and worked to lift that burden. Here on the mountain, the strain of their shared survival was lighter, and they were free to live.

Lettie allowed her hand to brush the square carton of Camel Lights through the pocket of her jeans. She wanted to smoke badly, to feel the nicotine dampen the flare of fear like water dissolved a stain. Instead, she folded her arms over her chest and walked faster up the trail. Most of Titan Mountain was hardwood forest, steep slopes and green gray rock. Small trails worn into the earth converged on the cabin like a web of veins to a beating heart. Most of the paths led to favorite hunting spots or dissipated altogether, but one curved up and over the peak. It led to a wide clearing next to a creek she and Tommy visited during their honeymoon. Lettie was surprised and pleased that she still remembered the way well enough to take Stella there.

The distance from the hunting cabin to the creek was not great, just a little over a mile, but Lettie was still exhausted when they arrived. The trail was steep, and several times she was forced to brace one arm against the ground or cling to a sapling for balance. Lettie could also feel the draw of life knitting itself together inside her. Unlike the weariness that came from overworked muscles or eyes reddened from lack of sleep, no amount of rest could ease the fatigue of creation.

"Mama, look, I can see the water."

"Stella baby, wait right there. Don't get in until I get there."

Lettie tried to quicken her pace and catch up to her daughter, but the steep downward slope of the trail pounded her already tired body and drove the bone of her leg into her hip. Stella bounced from one foot to the other, anxious to test herself against the cold of the mountain stream. Anxious as she was, the little girl still paused long enough to question her mother.

"Did Daddy live here before he died?"

Stella had never known her father. His death was a fact for her, a matter of history without the burden of lived pain. Lettie understood this, but in front of the homeplace the mention of him still hurt, stopped her breath.

"No, baby, your daddy never lived here, but he was here when he was your age. No one has really lived here."

"Why didn't daddy want to live here? I love it. Could we live here, mommy? I could help you clean it up. We could get some paint from your work to make the house pretty again."

"It would take more than paint, Stella. That old place doesn't have lights or running water."

"Oh. Well, I still love it. Where did Daddy like to play?"

Lettie never stopped being amazed by how quickly her daughter could switch from a small adult who offered plans to remodel the house to a child anxious to play. It seems that here on the mountain that change occurred more quickly and favored the child over the adult. If the absence of lights and an indoor toilet gave Stella the freedom to be a little girl, perhaps the cabin could be salvaged.

"He told me his favorite place was down there by the creek."

Stella's wide eyes followed the line of her mother's outstretched arm across the cleared area that surrounded the house to where the tree line began again. The promise of a new discovery and the chance to play in water prompted her to resume her dance.

"Let's go, Mamma. Can I get in the water now?"

"Sure, Stella. Roll up your pants first. We can eat lunch down there too. I made peanut butter and jelly."

Stella squealed and ran for the trees. Lettie followed at a much slower pace, winced as water from the tall wet grass soaked her lower legs. The strain of the hike from the cabin to the creek had prevented her from thinking about the fear that brought her to the mountain in the first place. On level ground again, the demands of her body retreated, made room for worry.

She was pregnant. In spite of the morning sickness and a constant desire to sleep, Lettie had not allowed herself to face what that meant. Under the best of circumstances another child was cause for panic. There was Pastor Lindt. Even though they slept together, she still couldn't call him by his first name. They had only been together once, but that was enough. Tommy was her first, and after he was killed, she he was too busy trying to provide for their daughter to have a man in her life. The idea of birth control never occurred to her, wasn't something she thought she needed.

Stella was already in the creek, pants rolled past her knees, arms out for balance when Lettie reached the steep bank. The winding vein of water wasn't deep, knee high on an adult, but the creek moved fast and strong. The swift run of water over the rocks made them as slick as the skin of newly bathed baby, making balance difficult. Lettie watched her daughter make her way along the creek bed, begin to slip on the rocks right herself with a hand plunged into the water, then move on. Lettie eased herself to the ground, put the My Little Pony backpack that held their lunch next to her.

"Be careful, honey. Those rocks are slick."

"I will, Mamma."

Lindt seemed kind at first. He visited her home unannounced after she attended Sunday worship for the first time. He asked her questions about Stella and about herself. Lindt walked through her home while they talked, looked at Stella's artwork on the refrigerator, the picture of Tommy next to the folded flag. When he asked her about her husband, something in his voice opened a wound in Lettie, like a scalpel over scar tissue, tearing more than cutting. She wept and told him everything. She talked about how young they were when they got married and how the explosion that killed Tommy meant his casket held only pieces of her husband. Lindt knelt and held her hands and prayed before he left.

*****

The remains of a barbed wire fence ran along the edge of the creek near where Lettie sat. The posts were split with age and faded to the color of ash. The wire sagged and was rusted, brittle brown. She watched a small gray bird, almost invisible against the fence post. The bird's head jerked side to side as it struggled to hold a writhing cricket in its too small beak. One blink swift motion of its feathered head down to the scaled point of the barb, and the bird flew. Lettie stood and walked a few steps to the fence post perch. The cricket's earthy black body was impaled down to the rough knot that bound the barb. She watched segmented legs kick against empty air, twist the shaft deeper through its broken body. She reached out to remove the bug but stopped. The damage was done, she could not change that, only deny the hunter's meal.

"Mamma, what are you looking at?"

Stella's voice drew her eyes away from the sacrifice, back to her water-washed child. "Nothing, baby. Come out of that creek. It's time to eat."

*****

Lindt extended the fingers of both hands and dug the flesh between thumb and forefinger into the ridges of the truck steering wheel. He had called Helen from Lettie's driveway and told her that he would not be home that night. He often retreated to the mountains and camped on an empty stretch of trail. Until he began to visit Lettie, Helen accepted his retreats, told him that "even Jesus needed time on the mountain to pray." Tyson knew that she was relieved to have him out of the house. This time was different. He could hear the suspicion in her voice, the undercurrent of anger. He needed to be quick, find Lettie and return home before Helen did something dangerous. Lindt had driven all night and found nothing.

He reached over and turned the radio up almost as high as it could go. Even the jolt of the late-night truck stop coffee began to fade. An evangelist from Tennessee shouted about sin from the static edge of the dial.

Lindt knew he was better than the voice that crackled over the mountaintop. If he could stop his life from falling apart, maybe he could find fame preaching to a congregation he couldn't see. Maybe that was the reason for this test. God was ready to bless him, open new doors if he could find his way through this wilderness and destroy the sin of the flesh. Lettie was nothing but sin.

The first time she walked into his church Tyson couldn't stop watching her. He preached longer and louder than usual, looked at her again and again. He was angry when she left early, led her squirming daughter out before the last hymn. That afternoon when Helen lifted her tent of a dress over her head and reached for his belt buckle, it was Lettie's hands that he saw. Tyson knew when she wept during his first visit to her home that he could have her whenever he wanted. Two visits later he did have her while the little girl played at a friend's house, whispering gently the entire time.

The truck's rear tire slipped on the edge of the road and pulled him awake and over the center line. He found Titan Mountain in the early hours of the morning. The GPS on his phone brought him as far as an empty exit off the interstate; after that he was on his own. There were few actual roads, and he followed several until they ended in dirt paths that led to sunken-in trailers. It was daylight now, and he began to realize the search was impossible. He would never find Lettie in the tangle of coves and ridges. If only she had been willing to take care of it like he asked. Lindt used the voice to explain to her that a child would ruin them both. He was surprised and angry when she refused. He hit her, hard in the face with the back of his hand. She didn't scream or even cry, just threatened to call the police. Lindt left, ran for the truck, drove home, and tried to appear calm in front of Helen while he waited for a sheriff's cruiser to appear in the driveway. The truck slipped again, this time threatening to slide off the narrow road into the ravine below. Lindt knew he was beaten, that deliverance would not come. If he continued the search, he would fall asleep and drop off the edge of the mountain. All he could do now was pull over and sleep in the truck until he was alert enough to drive and pray that Lettie never came back. A few yards ahead a dirt path ran at a ridiculous angle away from the road and up into the tree line. Lindt pulled in and turned off the ignition. His head was bowed over the steering wheel when he felt the pressure of the burnt coffee in his bladder. He slipped in the on the muddy path and sent a warm stream of urine over the toes of his shoes when he saw the set of wide tire tracks pressed into the dirt.

*****

The walk back to the cabin took longer than Lettie anticipated, and the sun had begun to climb down the mountain. Stella walked heavily in the purple light, a few steps behind her mother. Lettie was glad for the burn in her lungs and the ache in her hips. She was no closer to a plan that would unravel their trouble, and the pain made it easier to forget. She walked in hopes that tomorrow would bring a new revelation, a clear sign that pointed toward salvation.

"Mamma, I'm hungry. Can I have another pop tart when we get back to the tree house?"

Stella almost never whined, but there was a note of pleading in the little girl's voice that Lettie could not ignore. "Sure, little star, you can have a pop tart, but just one. I don't want you to spoil your dinner."

"Thank you, Mamma. Thank you. I promise just one." Restored by the promise of her favorite treat, Stella ran ahead squealing and clapping her hands.

Lettie moaned when her shoe caught on a rock on the trail and promised to break the blister that had formed under her toe, then laughed low as the hurt faded. Her pain and the signless world were un-important as long as Stella and the waiting child inside her were safe.

*****

Lindt waited for hours inside the cabin before he heard the girl's squeals. There was nowhere to conceal the truck, so he parked behind the Firebird to prevent any attempt at escape. Once inside the unlocked cabin, he sat on the cot where Lettie and the girl slept, lifted the quilt to his face and breathed deeply. His thoughts became fragmented, images without words, free of the controls of language. He saw Helen, her face melted in loose lines of rage, then the bare cell where he spent years of fear, never allowed him to fully sleep. Then there was Lettie as he saw her in church and later underneath him, eyes closed and face blank. One image moved him, broke his stillness. Lettie underneath him again, this time covered in blood. He needed a weapon, something to bring the blood, open the vein of blessing.

He searched the cabin, threw the contents of cabinets on the floor, overturned frail furniture. Lindt's hands remembered the desperate days of broken locks for hidden bills, weak with the need to get well. Upstairs there was nothing; his hands could feel the hate in the old boards, a refusal to yield to his hunt. He remembered the shadowed, stone-closed darkness below. In a corner, forgotten and rusted, he found a blade. The curved knife was dull, and the tip was broken from contact with animal bones. Lindt studied the stained steel blade. It was more than the flint wedge Abraham held, and the hand behind it was stronger, more sure.

*****

Lettie crested the small ridge, looked down on the cabin and the black truck when her daughter called out. "Mama, I think that preacher is here." Her knees melted as the word "how" began to form on her open lips. She saw Lindt step from the shadows under the cabin, saw the knife in his hand, his eyes on Stella. The car was between them, the firebird's one eye turned toward Lindt.

"Run, Stella. Now."

The little girl turned, too afraid to scream and ran toward her mother. All Lettie could see were her eyes wide with old known death. Lindt charged straight for the girl, collided with the car, fell, rolled, and righted himself. It was enough. Lettie grabbed her daughter's hand and fled back down the trail. Lindt behind them. Lettie could hear his footsteps and the rapid hiss of his breath. The fear from before was gone, replaced by Stella's sweat-slick hand in hers, flesh to flesh. He would catch them on the trail. Stella wasn't fast enough. They had to hide, hoped for shelter in the dark trees.

Lettie tightened her grip on her daughter, shifted her hand from palm to her fragile, bird-boned wrist. She stepped off the trail without breaking her stride. Away from the path, their feet whispered through past winter's leaf fall, sharp and high. Lettie whispered with their sound, "Run Stella. I have you. I won't let go."

Lindt saw mother and child leave the trail. The girl was small, weak. He would have them soon. Under his heavier stride the cloistered prayer of leaf fall whisper rasped harsh and angry. The knife was cold, slick in his palm, unyielding. He would kill the mother first. The girl would not go far.

Lettie could hear death behind her. They were still too slow, and there was nowhere to hide. In front of them the serpentine curve of ink-black water stopped. The creek was wide, steep sides and rock scales. Lettie lifted her daughter, an arm around the child's waist. She pressed her face into the girl's hair, smelled the sweat. "Don't stop, Stella. No matter what, don't stop." She swung her hips to try to let go, arc the little body over the darkness, but Stella held on, would not be saved.

"Mamma, no." The impact was hard, snapped her neck to the side, then cold and sharp, stone against ribs. He was on top of her tangled legs in the dark water, hands on her throat, forcing her down. "Don't hurt her, please don't hurt her."

The knife was gone, slipped free in the short fall into the creek, but he didn't need the blade. His hands and the water were enough. The cold numbed to his arms, soothed the scratches the woman made as he pushed her under. She spoke. He heard the sound but didn't understand. There was no language, no voice in him.

Lettie dug fingers into the flow, into flesh, tore toward his bone, but it was beyond her reach. Water filled her mouth, throat, still she fought. Stella could still run, still hide if she made her dying last. One star in the dark would be hard to find, could cover light with shadow.

The weight lifted, her strained body pushed up, broke the surface. She choked, vomited water and felt small hands on her face. Lettie opened her eyes, saw Stella, wet and trembling pushing into her arms. The man was face down, one hand clinched, then never opened. The knife was in his neck, curved away from the base of the skull like the fan fin of a sea serpent.

"Stella, look at me."

The words grated raw from her the throat. The child refused to move at first, trembled against Lettie's chest. She cupped the small face, lifted the eyes and expected tears. The only tears were her own, seared and angry. Stella's eyes were dry, cold, far away. "I had to, Mamma. He was going to hurt you." Lettie pressed her face back into her chest, looked away. "I know baby, I know."

With Eyes to See

Marcus Dunn Hartley was sweating heavily under the old army issue raincoat that extended well past his knees. Manufactured in an era before breathable fabrics, the rubber-coated canvas trapped all the wearer's body heat. The sunlight on the outside of the coat left him damp in an atmosphere of his own making. The coat was uncomfortable, but it was reliable. His father had weathered more than a few violent rainstorms in the ancient slicker while repairing downed powerlines for Western Carolina Electric. The storms that blew through the mountains were often sudden and violent, leaving flooded creeks and fallen trees that meant long nights for the men employed by the power company.

Marcus had watched his mother retrieve the coat from the peg where it hung in their small cabin more times than he could count during his childhood. She would insist that his father wear it, though there was not cloud in the sky. Mamma always knew when it was going to rain. Daddy would have known that had he grown up in Mayesville and been familiar with the Dunn family's strange gift for predicting the movements of nature, but he didn't. It had only taken a few rain-soaked days of being caught in unforeseen showers before he believed what the old folks in town already knew. The Dunns were weather sharps. At least some of them were.

For as long as anyone could remember, there had always been a sharp in the Dunn family. Some of the ability came from simply being attentive. Harsh weather always sent forth heralds for those with eyes to see and ears to hear. Smoke rising from wood stoves and sinking to the ground or an abundance of fur on caterpillars were signs of a harsh winter. The nesting of birds and the thickness of morning fog were signs of thunderstorms. But there was more to the weather sharp's gift than folk science. Sharps saw connections, felt tremors in living things that ordinary folks missed, and the gift went far beyond predicting the weather. Though most kept it to themselves, it was impossible to lie to a weather sharp. Bodies gave away the truth when words concealed it. The speed of fingers raked through hair or the direction of a tongue over teeth were signs of a secret. The Dunns could see death, though most chose not to. The signs differed from one person to the next, but the span of every life could be read like rings in the trunk of a felled oak tree. More than a few sharps had gone crazy or turned to the bottle after discerning the death of a loved one unintentionally. Marcus' mother had always said that she married his daddy for two reasons. When he said he loved her, she knew he was telling the truth, and the taste of their first kiss promised that he would outlive her.

****

Marcus never learned to manage his foreknowledge as well as his mother. The ability to read the secrets of every person he encountered made him unable to spend much time in human company. The men in his family with the gift were always seen as strange, preferring to live alone in isolated cabins hidden in mountain hollows. Marcus lived in one of those cabins himself, on a piece of old family land.

Try as they might to hide from the world, the Dunn family hermits found that the world would come to them. Neighbors who knew of their strange gifts came to ask advice on when to plant a crop, begin construction on a new home, or what to do for a sick child. These visits were brief and the advice paid for with a sack of flour, a smoked ham, or some other necessary item. That was generations ago. He could go weeks or more without seeing another human being. If some visitor found their way to his cabin, he would likely have fled in terror from the bearded, snarling figure that came to the door. The gift was dying out because those who possessed it simply could not abide human contact long enough to pass on their strange genetic material. There were, however, some instances when pure carnal instinct overcame the cold surety of foreknowledge.

Following a flight of migrating monarch butterflies as they were battered by the wind, the patriarch of the Dunn family left his remote cabin and came to town. Gran Dunn introduced himself to the woman who would become his wife in a shower of spiraling wings ripped from fragile bodies. Creation never lied to those who knew how to listen.

For Dunns with the gift of foreknowledge, the first story of the Bible always held an excess of meaning. It was knowledge that led to expulsion from paradise, and generations of Dunns had been fleeing ever since. Great-great-great-grandfather Dunn's night of passion with Miss Lucy Thompson was on the one hand a refusal to succumb to original sin. Knowing too much kept Dunns from carrying on the family line. Lucy's father, Rev. Silas Thompson, had disagreed. Steeped in Methodist discipline, he knew base animal lust when he saw it. Marcus could have cared less if the tension in his stomach was the result of inspired resistance to original sin or a slide down the great chain of being.

Pressing his fists into the pockets of his raincoat, Marcus muttered, "I just want to get my damn check and go home." The combination of the unseasonable raincoat, wild hair, and self-directed mumbling gave him the appearance of a homeless person long off his medication. He didn't care what the tourists shopping for overpriced folk art thought about him. If they could look from face to face and predict everything from a toothache to cancer, they would look crazy, too. Or at least they would have stayed home in Florida. Not caring did not help him hate coming into town any less. Once a month he made the journey to the post office where he rented the smallest box available.

Inside the box, always on the first of the month, was the check he received from the government as consolation for his disability. The check had been his brother Levi's idea. Concerned for his "little" bother's ability to care of himself, the older of the twins by less than a minute forced Marcus to see a psychiatrist. According to the doctor, he suffered from mild paranoia, delusions of varying severity, severe social anxiety, and moderate agoraphobia. The conclusion of all those disorders and delusions was that Marcus would never be able to sustain a job or support himself.

Marcus kept silent throughout the session and refrained from pointing out that the lines around the doctor's mouth were a sure sign that his much younger wife was unfaithful. Marcus knew he wasn't crazy and was more than capable of supporting himself, but he didn't mind the monthly check.

Check in hand, he made his way out of the post office and across the main street that was becoming uncomfortably crowded. Narrowly avoiding an on-coming pickup truck, he approached one of two banks, selected for its proximity to the post office. The bank was another of his brother's attempts to secure his quality of life. Marcus had protested at first, fearing that he would be forced to stand in line with other patrons and ultimately speak to a teller in order to deposit his money. Only after he was shown to the ATM on the side of the building did he cease to complain. He had little use for technology and did not even own a television, but he had to admit this was a convenience. With the money safely deposited, Marcus steeled himself for the most trying part of his monthly sojourn among humanity.

Along with the routine of retrieving and depositing his stipend, Marcus was required by his brother to attend a prayer service at St. Brigid's Catholic Church. Marcus had only once neglected to attend the service. Within an hour Levi was at his door, frantic and demanding to see if he was taking his medication. Marcus hated the pills more than people, and so he never missed another service. St. Brigid's was as much a Dunn family tradition as measuring the circumference of hickory shells to determine the duration of winter.

Gran Dunn, as later generations would call him, had known that his night with Miss Lucy would produce a child. He also knew that her father would not consent to marry them until her condition became more obvious and embarrassing. Unlike his teetotalling Protestant counterpart, the priest at St. Brigid's was known to take a shot of whiskey or sample the product from a parishioner's still from time to time. He was also known to be deeply tolerant of his parishioners' moral failings provided that they attended Mass and made confession on a regular basis. Gran Dunn had appeared at the priest's cottage well after midnight and asked the aging but spry priest to perform a wedding on the spot. Father McConnell, whose days' growth of white beard and well-worn bed clothes gave him the appearance of a potato left too long at the bottom of the bin, had consented with one provision. Gran and Lucy were married and baptized in the Roman Catholic Church on the same night. When protests later arose over Lucy's hasty conversion, Father McConnell would later claim that due to the late hour and his failing eyesight, he had not recognized the daughter of his ministerial colleague. It was never clear what angered Rev. Thompson more, the wedding or the baptism. Since that night, the doors of St. Brigid's had rarely opened without a Dunn in attendance.

Though the tiny Gothic church had been a mainstay in the life of their family, Marcus' brother took their commitment to new heights. The week before their high school graduation, Levi announced that he wanted to enter the priesthood. His parents had been pleased, but there was an undercurrent of disappointment with their eldest son's choice of vocation. They wanted to become grandparents, a hope that was now all but gone. Less than a week after his brother's departure for seminary in Boston, Marcus moved to the old cabin. Two decades later, Father Levi Dunn Hartley returned to preside over the Eucharist in the cradle of his faith.

Considered both young and handsome, Levi was beloved by his aging parish. It also did not hurt that he was a hometown boy who exhibited the most sacred of Appalachian virtues, loyalty to family. Following his parents' deaths, Levi had given up a prestigious teaching position at a Catholic university to return home and care for his unstable brother. What few people knew was that his mother had informed him on exactly what day both she and their father were going to join the Church Triumphant. Both had died in their sleep, quite possibly within minutes of one another.

Marcus was crouched in the church yard when his brother spotted him. "What are you doing rooting in the dirt, little brother? And why are you wearing that rain jacket? There isn't a cloud in the sky."

For a moment Marcus ignored his brother's booming voice and kept his attention on the colony of ants that made their home beneath a large hemlock in the church yard. The ants were carefully sealing up the entrance to their mound, another sure sign of a sudden rainstorm.

"Levi, why do you make me do this? You know I hate it."

Reaching down and placing his hand under his brother's arm, Levi whispered, "I make you do this because I love you and it is good for you. No one needs to be alone all the time."

Marcus looked into his brother's broad face that had once been an exact mirror of his own and knew that he was telling the truth. The slight arch of his eyebrows and the straight set of his mouth were as clear an indicator of honesty as the ants were of rain. There was something else there too, but Marcus looked away before he could discover more than he wanted to know. He knew his brother loved him and in forty-two years had never lied to him.

"Fine. I will come inside, but you had better make it quick this time. A bad storm is coming, and the road to the cabin gets rough when the creek floods."

Looking into his brother's eyes while maintaining the gentle grip on his bothers arm, Levi said, "Little Brother, there is nothing but sun overhead. It isn't going to rain."

"You know better than to put any stock in what is overhead. Those ants know what is coming even if you don't."

Guiding his brother gently through the church door, Levi continued to whisper as if talking to a frightened animal, "We'll see, little brother, we'll see."

Walking into St. Brigid's always made Marcus feel as if he was staring through the bottom of one his mother's colored glass ashtrays. The walls were made from the same dark stone as the surrounding mountains. The Scot stonemasons who assembled the church had paid careful attention to the irregular shape of each stone as they joined them together. Not a single one had been cut or chiseled. Instead, they were carefully gathered from fields and riverbeds and fitted together as they were. The only natural light that entered St. Brigid's was filtered through stained-glass windows old as the church itself. Six of the windows extended from floor to ceiling and lined the church, each one depicting a different scene from the Gospels. The seventh was round and occupied most of the wall behind the black slate altar.

The final window showed the crucified savior hanging limp on the cross. His side had just been pierced by the legionary's spear, and a bright blue flow of water issued forth. Marcus never doubted the account of an earthquake that followed Jesus' death. The black lines, carefully painted to give the water the appearance of motion, flowed in a direction that was a sure sign of natural disaster.

Marcus slouched into a rear pew careful to avoid eye contact with the other worshippers. He slid as far from the center aisle as he could manage and he began to run his fingers over the worn pew cushion. He found a familiar tear along one of the seams. Levi had made the incision decades ago with a smuggled pocketknife. Even as a child, Marcus struggled to be in the company of people other than his family. Church had been particularly difficult as everyone made an effort to be friendly even to a child as painfully shy as he had been. Though toys were strictly forbidden by his parents in church, Levi had hidden a pair of plastic soldiers in the cushion for his brother. Just having the soldiers to run his fingers over had made it easier to endure the presence of bodies other than his own.

The already quiet church fell completely silent as Levi's near perfect tenor voice began to chant the opening psalm. Without pausing, he lit a bowl of incense on the altar, and the scent of frankincense and myrrh began to drift over the congregation. Marcus watched as the smoke struggled to rise. Another sign that was rain was coming.

Sliding gently from the last note of the psalm into regular speech, Levi directed the congregation to a page in the Missal. Looking up for the first time, the congregation fumbled for the prayer books beneath their seats. Some of the older folks he recognized from his childhood. Seated near the front, bent with age and arthritis was Eunice Tybee. Frustrated by his refusal to speak during her catechism class, she had tormented him as a child, calling on him more than any other student. Most of the time Levi came to his aid, but on one occasion she refused to allow him to be rescued. She forced the class to sit in silence and wait for his answer. Marcus was shy but he was no coward. Speaking just above his normal whisper, he explained to Miss Tybee that "her cold would go away if she would stop smoking cigarettes." The class exploded with laughter, and Eunice had turned scarlet with rage and embarrassment. Class was dismissed early, and Marcus was never called on for an answer again.

Seated next to Eunice was her youngest daughter, Margaret. The younger Tybee had been considered quite the beauty when she had attended school with Marcus and Levi. Her good looks had not prevented a bitter divorce that brought her home from Atlanta to live with her mother. Marcus did not need the gift of foresight to see why she faithfully attended the daily praying of the hours with her mother. She never took her eyes off Levi. The sound of falling leaves came to a stop as a dozen pairs of hands found their place in the pages of the prayer book. Levi's voice began the words of the confession and was quickly joined by the others, "I confess to God Almighty, before the whole company of heaven, and to you, my brothers and sisters…"

Marcus dropped his head and gripped the pew in front of him with both hands. The service was always the same. A psalm followed by a prayer of confession. It was meant to be a moment of truth that led to forgiveness. Marcus knew better. He knew if he watched the movements of shoulders, the tilts of necks, he would see the emptiness of the words. Behind the steady drone of the prayer, he could hear another sound building. A gentle tap on the windows quickly became a heavy rattle against the brittle stained glass. He looked up and watched as the first streaks of rain took on the color of blood against the crimson windowpanes.

"That I have sinned in thought, word, and deed; in what I have done and what I have failed to do…"

All the familiar signs were there. The mouth shaped like a secret, a hint of resentment in the tilt of his brother's neck. There was also something else. It reminded Marcus of the fog that settled on the mountaintops and remained sometimes until midday. Even up close it was impenetrable hiding everything but the nearest objects. Marcus often walked in those resting clouds, letting the damp air settle into his beard and hair until it ran in streams over his face. His gift made him so tired, always assembling signs until they revealed a whole story. In the fog, nothing connected or collided. Marcus looked from face to face in the little church. It was the same for all of them. The creases carved out by anger, shoulders bent with failure. It was all still there. Their voices, pitched low in prayer-bound unison, softened the certainty of the signs. For the first time, he could remember it did not hurt to see them.

The prayer ended with his brother's extended arms. The voices scattered into their own rhythm on the amen. The liturgy continued on, but Marcus looked away, toward the stained-glass window. He watched as the heavy raindrops fell on the crowd gathered at the painted feet of Jesus. He kept his eyes fastened on their perpetually upturned faces until the creaking of wood signaled that people were rising to leave. Once the faithful had been shepherded out the door, Levi slipped into the pew next to his brother.

"It looks like you were right about the rain, little brother. It's coming down in buckets out there."

"I'm always right about the rain."

Levi nodded and said, "You should probably head home before the road to the cabin gets too washed out."

Marcus rose quickly and pressed past his brother, anxious to put an end to sojourn among humanity. He paused at the end of the pew and looked back at Levi. Slipping out of the raincoat, he folded it onto his brother's lap.

"Take this, big brother. It will be awhile before the rain stops."

Lost And Found In East Jesus

The naked man brushed dirt from his bare knees and extended his hand. James had never shaken hands with a nudist before. Male nudity made him uncomfortable even in a setting where bare flesh was to be expected. He always rushed through his dressing routine at the YMCA, unwilling to banter in the buff the way some of the other men in the locker room did. The man's hairy body and taut swell of stomach, displayed out of doors and in broad daylight, alone would have been enough to make James uneasy, but there was more. On top of his bare head the naked gardener who just seconds ago rooted in a patch of desert soil, was topped by a pair of plush rabbit ears. Held in place by a pink plastic head band, the white ears were tattered and stained, faded in spots to a pathetic shade of abused grey. The area below his waist was equally decorative. Long chords in a variety of colors were braided into ample pubic hair. At the end of each cord was a bottle cap that clinked against its fellows when the man stood, made the music of a pornographic wind chime. James took the offered hand, careful to make steady eye contact with the man who spoke in a cheerful bellow that reminded him of a department store Santa Claus.

"You must be Darryl's friend. I've been waiting for you. My name is Ellis, but the Slabbers call me Bunny. Welcome to East Jesus."

James ended the handshake as quickly as possible and forced himself not to wipe the transferred grit on his nylon hiking pants while Bunny watched. Outside the sterile air-conditioned cockpit of his Lexus SUV, the heat was immediate, almost violent. Concerned about dehydration, he consumed three bottles of imported water during the ninety-minute drive from Apple Valley, but he still felt lightheaded. The naked rabbit wasn't making any sense. Was this heat stroke so soon? James decided to start with what he knew.

"My name is Dr. James Masterson. I am here looking for my friend Dr. Darryl Watersby. We are business partners. He told me he was living in Slab City, but you said this is East Jesus. I followed the GPS in my car, and it brought me here. Am I in the right place? Darryl didn't know I was coming."

"Brother, no wonder you're confused. All that GPS business is nothing but a government conspiracy to track anyone they want. You still made it to the right place though. East Jesus is what you might call a suburb of Slab City or a borough if this were New York City. I know Darryl, but he never said anything about being a doctor."

Bunny laughed when he delivered the line about New York and caused the bottle caps to sing below his waist. James kept his eyes up, but his stomach recoiled with the effort. He would have preferred to avert his eyes from the telltale of a rattlesnake than Bunny's body art.

"Dr. Watersby and I share an optometry practice in Apple Valley. We've been partners for almost fifteen years. He came down here after his wife left. He called me pretty regularly until about a week ago. I was concerned, so I decided to drive down here and see if he was all right, but I didn't tell him I was coming. Do you know where I could find him?"

One hand reached up to adjust the rabbit ears that had begun to slide down his sweat-slicked forehead while the other scratched his ample gut. "I haven't seen Darryl in a few days, but I know someone who might know where to find him. You need to meet Rev. Starnes. Come on. I'll take you to the church."

Bunny turned away from James, confident that the other man would follow in his unshod footsteps. James' stomach tightened again when presented with an opposite view of his guide. Tattooed across Bunny's backside was the image of a magician in the act of sawing his assistant in half. The crack of the man's ass provided the line of separation in the illusionist's box.

James followed Bunny, a few uncomfortable steps behind, kept his head turned to one side, and took in the landscape around him. Other than his naked guide, there were no signs of life, but it was obvious that people did live here. Trailers in various states of disrepair and styles were settled in a random pattern, most nestled against the few stunted trees that grew in the desert landscape. In addition to the trailers, there were numerous sculptures, though James felt that was a generous term for the piles of trash heaped into roughly recognizable shapes. The largest of the artworks appeared to be a crucifix of some kind, the body formed from old tires and hub caps. The head of the crucified savior was made from a broken television set, the screen replaced with a hand-lettered sign that read, "Believe, but not everything."

"The church is right over there. I'll get the Rev's attention for you so he'll know you're all right, but I can't go inside. He won't let me in when I'm buffing it, but I can't put on clothes before noon. Pastor is a good guy, but we have a few theological differences. He doesn't have the same appreciation for the human body that I do."

It came as a comfort to James that there was at least one other person in this place who shared his distaste for public displays of genitalia. If the preacher had turned out to be a nudist too, he wasn't sure he could stay. The idea of taking counsel with a naked priest disturbed him more than Bunny's bottle caps.

Bunny walked up a short flight of wooden steps to the door of a trailer painted the same light blue as the desert sky. Elevated as he was, James got another unwelcome view of the other man's tattoo, close enough this time to see that both the magician and his assistant winked at anyone unfortunate enough to observe their facial expressions. James turned away just as Bunny pounded the door, the sound of his fist against thin metal, harmonizing with the bottle caps.

"Hey, preacher, there's a lost soul out here who needs to see you. His name is Dr. James and he's a friend of Darryl's."

Footsteps sounded over a creaking floor before a voice spoke through the still closed door.

"Bunny, is that you."

"Yeah, Rev, it's me."

"Do you have clothes on?"

"I think we both know the answer to that, preacher."

"In that case get your naked ass off my front porch. It's too early in the day to have a grown man's business in my face."

"Does that mean it will be OK later?"

"Bunny, get off my porch. Tell our visitor to wait while I give you time to get gone."

"OK, Rev, but this isn't over. You'll come around to my point of you view eventually. God made this and said it was good."

Bunny laughed and slapped both hands against his bare stomach before walking down the stairs. He placed one hand on James' tensed shoulder and leaned in close enough to whisper in his ear before he walked away.

"Good luck, and I hope you find what you came here for. If you're still around later, stop by my place for a drink. I make the best appletini in the state of California."

He still shuddered from the proximity of Bunny's naked bulk when the door of the trailer cracked open and the voice from before spoke, this time addressed to James.

"Is that naked shit gone?"

"He's gone."

The door completed its circuit on sand-worn hinges, ground open like the entrance to a long-sealed tomb. The man who emerged was almost as disquieting to James as Bunny, though he was clothed. His dark hair and massive beard were streaked with white and interwoven to form a single massive corona around his upper body. Starnes was dressed in a white button-down shirt and cutoff blue jeans that revealed thin legs knotted with muscle. The disproportion between the man's expansive hair and sliver of a body reminded James of movie he had seen once. Severed heads were impaled on spikes as punishment for crimes he no longer remembered. Starnes walked down the steps of the trailer slowly, scanning the area as he went.

"Good. He's actually gone. The last time I told Bunny to take his bare ass off my porch he only pretended to leave. As soon I as stepped out my front door, he jumped out at me shaking his kibbles and bits and yelling 'glory, glory' at the top his lungs. Damn near ruined my breakfast. So, who the hell are you?"

The older man looked James directly in his eyes to ask the last question. He found it impossible to meet the other man's gaze for more than a few seconds. Starnes' eyes left him stripped bare, as if any answer he might offer was already known.

"My name is James Masterson. I came here to find my friend Darryl. Bunny said you might know where he is."

"Why do you want to find him?"

James raised one hand above his eyes to block out the headache-inducing glare from the sun, but also to give him time to formulate an answer to the other man's unexpected question.

"He's my friend. I haven't heard from him in almost two weeks. I want to make sure that he is all right."

Starnes leaned into James' face and breathed out a single word.

"Bullshit."

His breath smelled faintly sweet. James' stomach turned over from the warm scent nearly breathed into his own lungs.

"What do you mean? Why else would I drive all the way from Apple Valley?" James gestured toward the direction where he had last seen Bunny. "It sure as shit wasn't for the view."

Starnes grabbed a fistful of beard, reaching under it and behind. His fingers thrust out through the matted hair just long enough to give the impression that some sort of tentacled animal was about to emerge.

"Guys like you just don't come here, even for a friend. Especially for a friend. You want something. I can see it. Smell it too. Why are you really in the Slabs?"

There was no anger in the old man's words, or even judgment. If anything, he sounded almost mournful, like a man resigned to tragedy. If Starnes had shouted, pointed a bony finger in his face, James might have found it in him to lie. James stepped away, tried to clear himself of the old man's scent.

"You're right. I didn't come here only out of concern for Darryl. We're business partners. Half of our practice belongs to him. We still owe money on some of the equipment. If he doesn't get his shit together and come back, we could both lose everything. Darryl can't just take off to live like some kind of freak in the desert and leave me in the lurch like this. I need to find him and bring him home."

"That's more like it. I knew there was something else. Darryl said you would come and that he needed to be ready. He told me not to stop you from trying to find him."

"Then you do know where he is."

The old man hesitated before he answered, one hand still combing through the tangle of his beard. "Not exactly. Darryl came to me a few days ago in a bad way. He said he had an important decision to make, but he couldn't make up his mind. He wanted my advice on how to find an answer, but he wouldn't tell me what the question was. I told him that when I needed answers, I went to the desert to clear my head. I haven't seen him since."

James felt a wave of nausea turn his stomach. He took another step away, but the heavy sweet scent of Starnes' breath pursued him. At the same time the sun burrowed into and under his skin, burned him from the inside out.

"What do you mean he went into the desert? We're already in the damn desert. Where could he possibly go from here?"

Starnes laughed, and his scent filled the air like a living thing. "This isn't the desert, son. This is the Slabs. The real desert is out there."

James followed the old man's extended finger where it pointed into the distance. Beyond the scattering of trailers and piles of trash was an expanse of endless sand, white and shimmering with heat. Looking into the emptiness blurred his vision and made James feel as if he would go blind, but not before his eyes boiled in their sockets. He staggered toward the porch railing and rested his head against the sun-scorched wood.

Starnes dropped his arm but remained still. "You don't look so good. The heat out here can be rough if you're not used to it. Darryl's trailer is just the other side of the church. Why don't you go over there and lie down, maybe drink some water? I know you'll find Daryl when the time is right, though I suspect it might be better for you if you didn't."

James was too sick to give much thought to the wild holy man's answer. He tried to step away from the porch railing and stand on his own, but the feeling of vertigo was too much. Water consumed in the cool comfort of his car rose in James throat and forced him to his knees.

He vomited onto the sand. The last thing he felt before he passed out was the coarse hair of Starnes beard brushed over his face like a woolen veil.

*****

Bunny leaned in close and inspected James' eyes before he pinched the skin of his forearm and let it drop. He performed the assessment while balancing a long-stemmed glass filled with translucent green liquid, a sliced apple suspended on the rim, in his free hand. Bunny still wore the degraded rabbit ears, but his bulk was now covered by a purple bathrobe marked by an L.A. Lakers logo above his heart. The robe gaped open and gave James a close-up view of Bunny's hair-covered chest through his pried-open eye.

"You can sit up now if you want, but take it slow. You've been out for a while."

James sat up slowly, gently rotated his body until his feet touched the floor. Bunny was right, he did feel weak and his skin tingled, but the nausea and dizziness were gone. He looked around the trailer, careful to keep his eyes from resting on Bunny. The interior of the Airstream was immaculate. There was even a framed photograph of James in a hard hat, one arm around Darryl, who leaned against a shovel. The picture was taken the day they broke ground on the office in Apple

Valley. Nothing suggested a man who was losing his mind.

"What happened?"

"The heat got you. Don't feel bad, though. It happens to a lot of first-timers in the Slabs. When you passed out, the Rev came and got me, and we brought you in here. If you're feeling up to it, we can head over to my place and get something to eat. A little food you in your stomach should set you right."

James stood up and felt a moment of panic when his knees refused to tighten in support of his weight. Before he could respond to the sensation in his failed limbs, Bunny was beside him, one hand on James' elbow. Before he collapsed, James would have pulled away from Bunny's touch, but weakness made him grateful, and his fingers curled into the loose terry cloth of the bathrobe. Careful not to move too quickly, Bunny guided his patient toward the door of the trailer, making low hums of encouragement with each step. Outside, everything was dark and completely silent.

James turned to Bunny and watched as the other man fumbled in the pockets of his robe for a small flashlight.

"I thought other people lived here. Where is everyone? There aren't even any lights on."

"There are plenty of other people around," Bunny answered as he guided them by the beam of the flashlight, which by some miracle of dexterity he held in the same hand as the martini glass. "Normally, they would be out celebrating another sundown, but the border patrol requested a blackout tonight. We Slabbers do what we can to be good citizens."

"What do you mean a blackout?"

"Slab City is fairly close to the border with Mexico. Coyotes sometimes pass this way with folks trying to sneak into the U.S. Every now and then they ask us to turn out our lights so their helicopters can spot movement in the desert. At first, there was a lot of argument about what we should do, but, in the end, most everyone decided we didn't want any trouble with the government. When the Border Patrol calls, the lights of Slab City go out."

Each step was easier than the last, and by the time the pair passed the darkened church, James was able to release his grip on Bunny's arm. Before he let go, James briefly tightened his grip on his companion's forearm.

"Thanks, Bunny. I think I've got it from here."

The two men walked on in the darkness. James followed a few steps behind Bunny, who led the way with his flashlight. Following the robed nudist into the dark of the desert was not something James would have imagined doing even a few hours ago, but something had loosened his constraint. Submission to this place had become a form of survival. James' eyes were so firmly fastened on the beam of light that he ran into Bunny, who had stopped just a few steps ahead him.

"Do you see that?"

Close contact with Bunny's covered but still tattooed lower half, threatened to restore his disgust, but James managed to bite back his hostility.

"Bunny, I can't see anything at all."

"Oh, sorry. How about now?"

He turned off the flashlight and grabbed James' chin to turn his head. At first, he saw nothing, only dark sky and stars. Just as he was about to free himself from Bunny's grip, James spotted what held his companion's attention. On the horizon and growing steadily closer was a constellation of lights, red and green, that pulsed as they dipped up and down. There was no sound to accompany the approach of the lights, but as they closed on the two men and passed overhead, there was a rush of wind and the impression of a dark winged shape as if an avenging angel stalked the desert sky. James and Bunny turned in perfect unison to follow the shadow as it past overhead. As they, watched flames appeared in the sky. The burning light grew suddenly brighter, arched up high, then plunged down into the void beyond Slab City.

"It's a sign. We have to follow it. I can feel it. If you want to find Darryl, we have to go now."

"What the hell are you talking about? We don't even know what that was, and there is no way it had anything to do with Darryl. What about the Border Patrol? We can't go running around in the desert when the entire town is on lockdown."

Bunny stopped his frantic tugging and stood perfectly still. He lifted the flashlight within inches of his face; the twin points of the plush ears illuminated from below looked like flares pointed toward the sky.

"This is bigger than the government. That was fire in the sky man, the oldest sign in the book. It doesn't matter how it got there. What matters is that we follow it. If we don't, there will be consequences. You can count on that. Besides, we won't be running off into the desert. We will be riding in style. Now come on. We have to hurry."

James thought his arm was going to be pulled from the socket this time when Bunny grabbed him and towed him into the darkness. He barely had time to wonder exactly what book of signs Bunny meant.

*****

Bunny whooped with drunken joy as their vehicle launched a few feet into the air and plowed down into the sand, propelled upward by a rise in the dunes. James held onto a metal bar next to the passenger seat and tried not to notice the effects of speed and gravity on Bunny's robe. If pressed, he would have called the vehicle a dune buggy, but it felt more primitive than that; just a pair of salvaged seats strapped to a metal frame, motor, and oversized tires. A pair of headlights bolstered by a row of spotlights welded to the roll bar above their heads illuminated the sand in front of the vehicle for no apparent purpose. There were no obstructions to avoid or a road to follow, just rolling sand. It was impossible to know how long they had been driving or in what direction they moved other than Bunny's declaration that they were following the flames in the sky.

James opened his grit-sealed eyes when the buggy fishtailed to a stop.

"I knew it. Holy shit, I knew it. A sign."

Bunny's mouth hung open as wide as his robe. From the top of the dune where they stopped, James saw flames that burned white at the center and pale blue where they reached into the sky. At the center of the fire was a broken wingspan that appeared to melt as he watched. Standing at almost equal distance away on the opposite side of the crash was a man that James knew must be Darryl.

"Turn off the car, Bunny. We'll walk from here."

The man stayed perfectly still, staring into the flames as the pair circled wide around the crash site to avoid the intense heat. James had imagined himself shouting at Darryl, berating him for abandoning their practice, but as he took a place at his friend's shoulder and joined his vigil over the wreckage, he found himself unable to speak. Darryl spoke first through cracked lips, his voice raw.

"Is that you, Bunny?"

Bunny replied in the fearful whisper of a child in church, "Yeah, man. It's me."

"I didn't recognize you with clothes on."

Bunny never took his eyes from the flames as he shifted his shoulders and let his robe fall in a heap at his feet.

"Is that better?"

"Yeah. Now you look like yourself. Hello, James. I knew you would get here sooner or later."

James looked first at Darryl then to Bunny. His partner looked like something from a survival film or an escaped convict. He was dressed in clothing almost identical to James, lightweight hiking pants and a nylon hiking shirt, but they were stained and torn, the pants ripped halfway up one leg. His hair was matted to his head, and a ragged beard clung to his face in sweat-caked slabs. Bunny was back in his natural state, bottle caps dangling free, the scandalous ears erect on his bald head. They belonged here. In this strange place bowed down before a flaming drone, Bunny and Darryl made sense. The wrongness of it filled James with rage. It wasn't fair. They should be ashamed for him to see them like this, apologetic for their disgusting oddity, but instead he felt like the intruder. He turned to Darryl and unleashed his rage.

"Damn right, you knew I was coming. We had a plan, a purpose. We invested years of our lives and everything we own into that practice, and you decide on a whim to come live like a bum in the desert with a bunch of freaks. What choice did I have but to come down here and bring you home? This isn't about you or your nervous breakdown, Darryl. It's my life too, and I don't want to spend it looking at Bunny's balls and bottle caps."

Darryl didn't respond to the anger in his partner's voice. He just spoke in low tones into the fire.

"I'm sorry you're upset, but I'm not coming back with you. I've made up my mind."

"I'm way past upset, you bastard. What about all the money we stand to lose if you keep this up. We will lose everything."

"James, I don't need any of that anymore, and neither do you. You just have to figure that out for yourself."

"Fine, you don't care about money. What about your reputation? What if you want to leave this shit hole one day and become a real person again? Do you think anyone will trust a doctor who lost his mind and ran off to the desert?"

"I am a real person here."

James clenched his fist at his side and fought the urge to punch Daryl in the mouth. He sensed that violence would only reinforce the other man's resistance. He took a forced deep breath and changed his tactic, then spoke in a soothing tone.

"You're exhausted, and from the look of it, you are dehydrated and starved. You're not thinking clearly. Come back to your trailer, get some fluids in your body, and we can talk about all of this later. Let me help you."

"I don't need food or water. I have everything I need right here. It's time for you to go, James. There is nothing else to say. Bunny will take you back to your car."

Though still soft and rasping, Darryl spoke the last words like a command. James no longer cared if he brought Darryl back or not. He wanted to hurt him, unleash on his flesh, and make the other man beg for mercy. James was about to reach for the other man's throat when a wash of light and a voice blasted from a loudspeaker stopped him.

"Step away from the vehicle and get down on your knees. That is the property of the United States government, and any tampering or theft is a federal offense. Do not resist, or we will use force."

James, Darryl, and Bunny all turned to face the direction of the voice and found themselves staring into several rows of lights so white they were nearly blinding and forced them to raise their hands to shield their eyes.

The voice echoed out again, bounced off the dunes, and their rib cages.

"Get down on your knees. This is your last chance to comply."

All three men dropped to sand, Bunny with a metallic rattle, and Darryl with a weakened groan. Only James was silent in his obedience. Their submission complete, they watched what at first appeared to be one figure that gradually separated into two emerge from the light. Lit from behind by the floodlights and from the front by the fire, the two Border Patrol agents seemed to glow from all sides, the badges on their tactical vests clearly visible. The agent on the loudspeaker stepped forward and spoke. His partner remained behind and to one side, perfectly silent.

"Who are you people, and what are you doing out here with my drone?"

Bunny spoke up first, as he extended his hands into the sky in a gesture of complete surrender.

"We weren't messing with you spy plane, officer. I swear it. Our friend here was just lost in the desert, and we were trying to find him. We don't want any trouble."

The agent's eyes widened when he turned to look at Bunny first, the man's decorated nakedness registering for the first time. The expression left his face with the practiced calm of someone trained to the horrors and oddities of the world. When he spoke next there was nothing in his voice to suggest that naked men wearing rabbit ears were not part of his daily routine.

"Are you trying to tell me that you just happened to find your lost friend next to my crashed aircraft, 'cause that sounds like a bullshit story if I ever heard one?"

Bunny raised his hands higher into the air and began to shake his head, the rabbit ears slipping forward with each twist of his neck.

"It's not exactly like that. We saw the drone crash and we followed it..."

Before Bunny could finish, Darryl groaned again and slumped forward face down in the sand. The silent agent stepped forward quick but not hurried and knelt down beside him. With practiced ease, he rolled Darryl's limp body over, checked his pulse and forced open one eye lid before he spoke to the other agent.

"Sir, this guy is in bad shape. He needs medical attention soon."

"Right now?"

"Yes, sir, right now."

The lead officer betrayed emotion for the first time as he ran a gloved hand over his face.

"Son of a bitch, could this night get any weirder? Get him up, and we'll take him to the hospital. I'll deal with these assholes."

He turned to James and Bunny as Darryl was lifted, still groaning, to his feet and half carried toward the waiting vehicle.

"I don't know why you two are out here and frankly I don't give a shit. If I write this up the way it happened, I will look as crazy as you two obviously are, so here's what's going to happen. I am going to take your friend to the hospital, and you two are going to leave the same way you got here. If you talk about this to anyone, I will arrest you for attempting to steal government property as an act of domestic terrorism. Hell, I might even claim you shot the damn thing down. Are we clear?"

Bunny stood, one hand raised in a sign of surrender, the other clutching at the back of James shirt dragging him to his feet.

"We are crystal clear officer. You will never hear from us again."

As they backed away, James felt the same rage as before the Border Patrol arrived. He shook himself free from Bunny's grasp and shouted in the direction the agent had taken Darryl.

"This isn't over. I will find you again. Count on it."

The agent stepped toward them, one hand dropping toward the pistol holstered against his thigh.

"What is he talking about? What isn't over?"

Bunny spun Darryl around and shoved him toward the buggy while he continued to back away.

"He's just worn out sir and worried about our friend. Don't pay any attention. We'll be on our way."

Bunny didn't wait for a reply. He turned and grabbed James by the shirt again, forcing both into a run for the waiting vehicle. Neither spoke for some time as they sped away from Darryl, the Border Patrol officers, and the burning drone. Bunny broke the silence as he looked down at himself in the driver seat.

"Damn, I forgot my robe. It was my favorite."

<<<<>>>>